EXPLODING ENDINGS

Books by Tim Harris

Exploding Endings 1: Painted Dogs & Doom Cakes
Exploding Endings 2: Dingbats & Lollypop Arms
Exploding Endings 3: Cursed Pants & Cranky Cops
Exploding Endings 4: Screenshots & Laughing Gas

Mr Bambuckle's Remarkables
Mr Bambuckle's Remarkables Fight Back
Mr Bambuckle's Remarkables Go Wild
Mr Bambuckle's Remarkables On the Lookout

Toffle Towers 1: Fully Booked
Toffle Towers 2: The Great River Race
Toffle Towers 3: Order in the Court

timharrisbooks.com

EXPLODING ENDINGS

Screenshots & Laughing Gas

TIM HARRIS

PUFFIN BOOKS

PUFFIN BOOKS

UK | USA | Canada | Ireland | Australia
India | New Zealand | South Africa | China

Penguin Random House Australia

Penguin Random House Australia is part of the Penguin Random House group of companies whose addresses can be found at global.penguinrandomhouse.com.

First published by Harbour Publishing House in 2017
This edition published by Puffin Books, an imprint of Penguin Random House Australia Pty Ltd, in 2020

Illustration, layout and cover design by Design For Days (designfordays.com)
Typeset by Harbour Publishing House.
Additional typesetting changes by Midland Typesetters, Australia.

Printed and bound in Australia by Griffin Press, an accredited ISO AS/NZS 14001 Environmental Management Systems printer

NATIONAL LIBRARY OF AUSTRALIA

A catalogue record for this book is available from the National Library of Australia

ISBN 978 1 76 089804 5

Penguin Random House Australia uses papers that are natural and recyclable products, made from wood grown in sustainable forests. The logging and manufacture processes are expected to conform to the environmental regulations of the country of origin.

penguin.com.au

CONTENTS

THE TOP 79 WEIRDEST THINGS TO TAKE TO SHOW-AND-TELL 7
SPIDER FLOSS 23
TANGENTINE TEXTS AGAIN 41
INTERPRETING MRS BLATCHFORD 56
SLOW LOTION 69
PAGE WARS (PART 1) 91
WANNA BUY THIS FOR FIVE BUCKS? 109
TANGENTINE TEXTS FOR A FAVOUR 125
SHORTCUT BURGERS 143
PAGE WARS (PART 2) 149
HIT 'EM HARD WITH A BACKYARD CARD 173
PAGE WARS (PART 3) 201
TANGENTINE TEXTS ONCE AGAIN 227

FOR JESS, MY INCREDIBLE SISTER

THE TOP 79 WEIRDEST THINGS TO TAKE TO SHOW-AND-TELL

1. Your grandma's false teeth. Especially if she hasn't cleaned them. Ever.

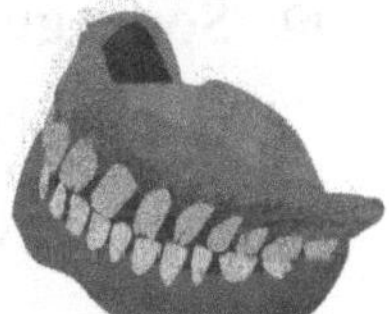

2. A drum kit that features built-in, volume-amplifying mega speakers. And twenty-five sets of ultra-enhancing hearing aids for your classmates.

3. The washing-up from the night before. *ask for an enthusiastic volunteer to give a real-life demonstration* *thank that person very much*

4. Your cousins. All thirty-seven of them.

5. The lamppost next to your letterbox. Random.

6. A close-up photo of you popping your first pimple.

7. The grass clippings from when you cut the lawn three Saturdays ago. The clippings you had to take out of the garbage bin near the back fence. The garbage bin that also contained your neighbour's dead cat. Those grass clippings.

8. Your pet axolotl's award-winning self-portrait painted in octopus ink. Even more random.

9. A real-life dragon, and sticks for your class to poke it with.

10. Some guy you met on the street last Tuesday and the enormous foam golf ball he was trying to balance on his head.

11. Your imaginary friend Stan and his imaginary friend Russell.

12. An inflatable dinghy. Inflated. And 25,000 litres of water.

13. Your very first nappy from when you were an innocent little baby who wouldn't dream of creating something so disgusting.

14. Your teacher's worst fear. *research heavily beforehand to ensure you get it just right*

15. The comet that is about to crash into the school. *claim the comet is your show-and-tell* *this will earn you the most incredible respect from your peers* *it may also get you expelled and end all life on earth*

16. A car park.

17. Sugary sweets and cans of soda for each of your classmates. *administer early in the day and enjoy watching your teacher lose control of everyone*

18. The love letters your dad wrote to your mum when they were dating.

19. A scrunched-up piece of paper from the garbage

bin next to your teacher's desk.

20. Earmuffs. *use them after show-and-tell to block out the noise of your teacher speaking*

21. A beached whale. *you may have to leave the beach behind as it'd be too heavy to carry* *mind you, you managed to bring the car park without any hassle* *throw in the beach for good measure and rally your classmates to help save the whale*

22. Speaking of wildlife – a wild bull. Make that an angry, wild bull. Also required are green shirts for your classmates and a bright red shirt for your teacher.

23. Your cold and flu symptoms.

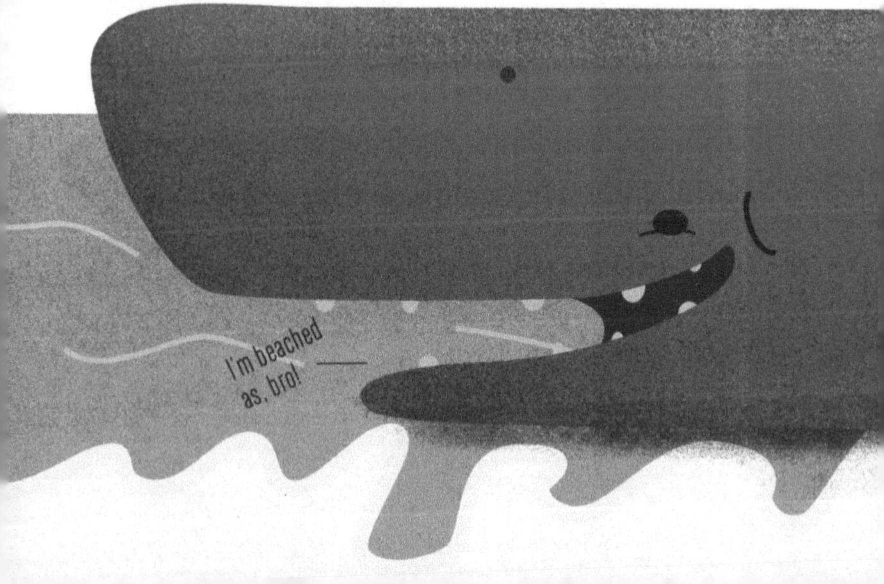

24. A dozen printed copies of your dad's boring work emails. *read aloud the first three so you cut into the Maths lesson*

25. A special electronic device that infiltrates the school's computer systems and sends out emails to all the parents announcing that the holidays are extended. Forever.

26. The Sydney New Year's Eve fireworks display.

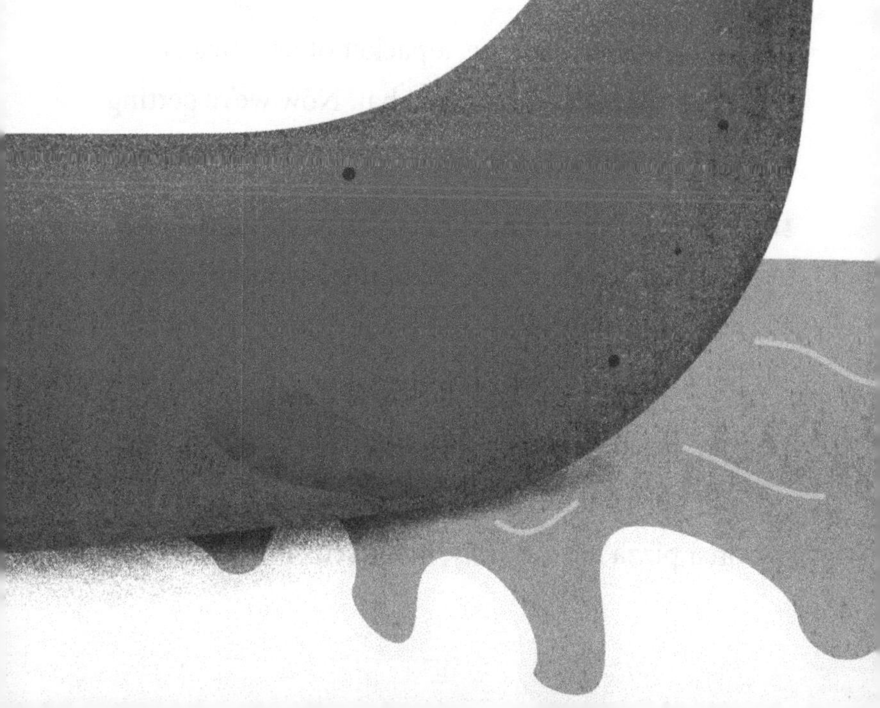

27. Nothing. Try winging it for a bit. See if anyone notices.

28. The Sahara Desert. Just make sure you don't get the sand mixed up with the sand from the beached whale's beach. I can't imagine how hard it would be for the poor whale to free itself from one of the hottest deserts on earth, not to mention the effort it would take your classmates to help free the whale. Mind you, you could give them the sugary sweets and cans of soda beforehand. That should give them the required energy levels. I can't believe how off-track we just got.

29. Laughing gas. Lots of it. Ha-ha-ha-ha!

30. An espresso machine, a packet of jelly beans, three goldfish and a safari hat. Now we're getting very random. Try linking those items together!

31. A cloud. I don't know how you're going to catch one, but have a crack. Bringing a cloud to school for show-and-tell would be awesome in anyone's book.

32. A new blend of sauce, halfway between tomato and barbecue. Call it 'Barbato Sauce' and try it on a pizza base. Surely, this needs to be invented.

You'll become rich and famous and host the best pizza parties ever! Your tastebuds will thank you. So will mine.

33. The entire contents of your sister's bedroom.

34. A hungry lion, a weak buffalo, a slow-motion camera and your best improvised documentary narration.

35. The Olympic Games. Good luck with that one.

36. The world's smallest watermelon and the world's largest grape. Compare the two. This will throw everyone's perception of size out the window.

37. A horse with an ice-cream cone stuck upside down on its head. *claim to have discovered unicorns* *eat the ice cream before strategically placing the cone*

38. Anti-adult spray. Enjoy a day without any grown-ups.

39. A burp in a jar.

40. A snow-making machine and some snowboards for your friends.

41. The little brown ball of goo that has been under your bed since you were three years old.

42. Your great-great-grandmother's delicate china bowl, and a heavy tenpin bowling ball. *carry the two items in the same bag for the sake of ease* *realising your error, visit an antique store on the way home* *buy a new delicate china bowl* *put it in a separate bag to carry home*

43. A portable camp fire, sixty delicious beef sausages, three loaves of bread and a bottle of 'Barbato Sauce'. *have a good story up your sleeve for the cooking process*

44. Tim Harris. He's weird.

45. Twelve drummers drumming, eleven pipers

piping, ten lords a-leaping, nine ladies dancing, eight maids a-milking, seven swans a-swimming, six geese a-laying, fiiiiive gooooolden riiiiings… four calling birds, three French hens, two turtle doves and a partridge in a pear tree.

46. An invisibility cloak. And invisibility socks in case your feet stick out. Harry never thought of that scenario.

47. A fire extinguisher. *demonstrate putting out a fire as if your teacher is ablaze*

48. A frisbee made out of dried cow dung.

49. Your uncle's monster truck.

50. The dead cockroach that has been under the fridge for the past couple of months.

51. A can of vegetable soup. Weird. I can't imagine you'd speak for more than fifteen seconds about that. I mean, what would you even say? '*This can of soup is very special to me. We've been friends for years. Sometimes, we play catch. I always win.*'

52. Your favourite movie, a popcorn maker, comfortable cushions, black curtains to block the light from the windows, a forty-inch wide-screen television and a letter from your parents saying that you have permission to combine the elements for your show-and-tell. *allow 90 minutes* *toilet break included*

53. A time machine so you can travel five minutes into the future and see how show-and-tell turned out. If it was a dismal failure, travel back into the past and choose something more interesting.

54. A giant snail and a saddle. Send your teacher on a ride around the neighbourhood. Conveniently, it will take your teacher about six days to return. *enjoy*

55. A thirty-one-centimetre ruler – just to annoy your friends.

56. A large mirror so the class just sits there staring at themselves during show-and-tell. *awkward*

57. Your atom collection. All four-hundred-and-seventy-nine billion, eighty-two million, six-hundred-and-fifty-three thousand and eleven of them.

58. A small fragment of air, the hole from a doughnut and a piece of the equator line.

59. An inappropriate full stop.

60. A jukebox containing really bad music from the 1980s. While your teacher is reminiscing for the next few hours, do whatever you want. *your teacher should snap out of it by the time *My Sharona* starts playing*

61. Your life-sized replica Tyrannosaurus rex.

62. A massive thunderstorm, and a warm raincoat for the classmate you have a crush on. Thunderstorms can be romantic, you know. *stay back to help your teacher clean up the mess* *what am I going on about? Don't stay back! Your teacher can deal with the mess*

63. An enormous slingshot. *open the classroom window and demonstrate by slinging your maths book to the other side of the world*

64. A powerful magnet that repels all classroom furniture. Shame, that.

65. Boy germs.

66. Your unopened lunchbox from the end of last year. *open it and enjoy the aroma*

67. A photoshopped picture of you as a baby racing a Formula One car.

68. Your mum's perfume collection and twenty-five pegs for your classmates' noses.

69. A giant hole puncher that enables you to put holes through entire books, desks and buildings. *be sure to empty the bottom out for interesting (and dangerous) confetti*

70. The tooth fairy and her collection of teeth. Actually, her collection of coins might be a bit more interesting.

71. Ask show-and-tell to come to you because you're too lazy to come to it.

72. A karaoke machine and microphone for your best friend to live out her dreams as a pop star. Make her sing some of that 1980s music your teacher listens to. While your teacher is distracted, find out how the whale you saved is doing.

73. Tangentine. Everyone wants to know what she looks like!

74. An empty ink cartridge. Try talking about it for longer than you did the can of vegetable soup. Let me know how you go! :)

75. The number seventy-five.

76. The anchor from a cruise ship. Point out how you borrowed it from the ship that is in the news

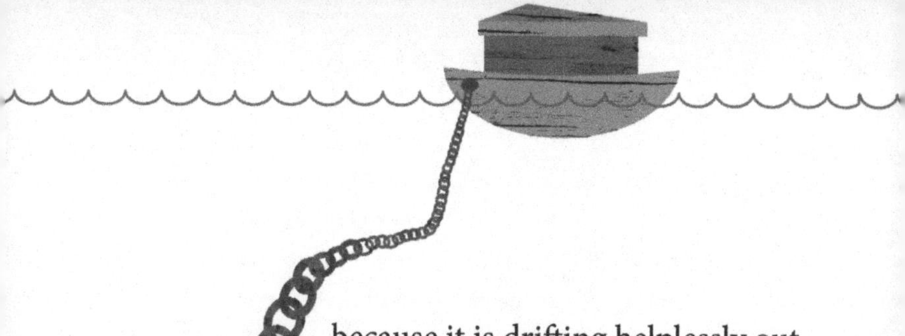

because it is drifting helplessly out to sea. *try to hide the anchor in your brother's room so he gets the blame*

77. The world's worst magician and some rotten tomatoes. You'll be in for an interesting experience, no matter what happens!

78. After arranging things with your teacher's parents, bring in a photo album from when your teacher was a kid. Claim the photos are yours. Watch the confusion on your teacher's face as you relive his or her childhood in your show-and-tell.

79. All of the above. At the same time.

SPIDER FLOSS

ONE

When Sir Howard Creame announced he would bc touring thc country to run a dessert-making competition, my whole life changed. It's not every day you get the chance to win a thousand dollars and a trip to Sydney to eat at his restaurant. Was I lucky to win the competition? Yeah, I guess you could say I was lucky.

Sir Howard Creame's Sydney restaurant is famous. People travel from all over the world to eat there. They fly in just to taste his desserts.

I've never eaten at his restaurant before. Yet, here I am, at the chef's table, being waited on like a movie star. I order his latest creation – an ice cream sundae in the shape of the Sydney Opera House. It costs more than a hundred dollars, but I get it for free. The waiter scribbles down my order and shuffles away like a penguin.

Sir Howard Creame pops out from the kitchen. He waves across to his fans and sits next to me. Everybody is staring at me. I bet they're jealous.

'Cindy, my dear, how delightful it is to see you again,' he says.

'Hello, Sir Howard,' I say. 'Thank you for choosing me.'

'A pleasure, a pleasure. I trust you enjoyed the flight. I insisted you travel first class, of course.'

'First class is cool,' I say. 'I've never sat at the front of a plane before.'

Sir Howard leans close to me. I can tell he wants to get down to business. 'I must know, dear Cindy, what is the name of your dessert? I simply *must* have the recipe.'

'Spider floss,' I say.

'Spider floss?'

'That's right.'

Sir Howard pulls a piece of paper from his pocket and puts it on the table. There is a large number written at the bottom of the paper. 'That's how much I am willing to pay you for your recipe,' he says. 'The spider-floss dessert will be our main attraction.'

It's hard not to hide my smile. 'Thank you,' I say.

Sir Howard leans closer still. 'Do tell me, Cindy. How did you create your dessert?'

'Pinko,' I say.

'Pinko?'

'Yes, Pinko.'

'What is Pinko?'

'Not *what* is Pinko,' I say. '*Who*.'

Sir Howard frowns. It's not an angry frown. It's a confused one. So, I tell him my story.

TWO

Everyone at school went bonkers when they found out Sir Howard Creame was coming to town. There was to be a competition like no other. Whoever made the best dessert had the chance to win a thousand dollars and a trip to Sydney. There was a lot of hype – just like that story about the man and his chocolate factory.

Sir Howard only gave a week's notice before he arrived in town. He said he didn't like giving anyone too much time to perfect a recipe. The best chefs, he said, delivered under pressure.

There was pressure, all right. Our town was announced as the last stop in his nationwide search – chances were he already had someone's recipe in mind.

I decided to work on a brownie recipe. Brownies can be delicious when they're done just right. And my brownies were up there with the best.

Lin and I talked about our ideas as we walked home from school.

'How will you make your brownies stand out?' Lin asked. 'I know a few others are making them, too.' Lin was a good friend like that – always pointing out problems.

'I haven't worked that out yet,' I said. 'But I'm sure I'll think of something.'

'I was going to make crème brûlée,' said Lin. 'But dessert is not my thing. I don't think I'll enter.' She stopped walking and pointed up. 'What's that?'

Hundreds of tiny pink threads floated across the afternoon sky. They looked like bits of string, drifting in the wind.

'No idea,' I said. And I didn't think about it again

until I got home and found a pink thread caught on my windowsill.

THREE

'I'm going to name you Pinko,' I said.

The tiny pink spider danced on the windowsill when I spoke. He seemed to like the sound of my voice. 'Pinko it is then.'

Pinko scurried outside and pulled on the pink thread of web that had carried him to my bedroom window. He dragged it inside and tied it to the bottom corner of the window, using it as the base of a new web, which he spun in a flash. He climbed into the middle of the web and blinked at me.

'You're a fast spinner,' I said. 'Nice web.'

Pinko bobbed up and down on the web and blinked again.

'I've gotta go and work on a recipe,' I said. 'I'll see you in a little while.'

The brownie recipe was coming along nicely, but I kept thinking about what Lin had said. How could I make it stand out? Sir Howard Creame wouldn't settle for any old dessert.

I tried mixing in berries. That made the brownies go soggy.

I tried adding extra chocolate. That made the brownies go hard in the oven.

I added more flour. That took away the flavour.

Nothing seemed to work. That was, until I thought outside the box.

'I've got it!' I said to Mum. 'I'm going to combine two of the greatest foods in the history of foodkind.'

'And what are two of the greatest foods in the history of foodkind?' said Mum, who had kindly let me take over the kitchen.

'Brownies and doughnuts,' I said. 'I am going to create the brownut!'

Mum's eyes sparkled. I could tell she liked the idea. 'I'll leave you to it, Cindy,' she said.

I spent the next few hours working on the right combination of ingredients. I had to get the balance just right. It couldn't be too much like a brownie, and it couldn't be too much like a doughnut.

It was almost dinnertime when I had perfected the brownut. It was shaped like a rectangle with a large circular hole in the middle. Although spongy like a doughnut, it was heavy like a brownie. I let Dad try it for his entree.

'It's delicious!' he cried. 'I want another one!'

'It's exquisite!' said Mum, who was more than happy to taste as well.

I took a bite out of my own brownut. Chocolate gooey goodness flooded my mouth. It was perfect.

'I'm going to take one to school to see what Lin thinks,' I said.

FOUR

Lin's reaction was even better than Mum's and Dad's. Her eyes widened at the first bite, and she squealed in delight. 'Cindy! This is the best thing ever!'

'I call it a brownut,' I said.

'Sounds stupid, if you ask me,' said Ryan Rattle. He was standing behind us.

Ryan Rattle was known for his bullying. He was always bossing kids around and calling them names. He was in my class and was usually the cause of any trouble.

'You wouldn't know delicious if it bit you on the bum,' said Lin. 'Here, try some.'

Ryan snatched the brownut from Lin's hand and shoved it in his mouth. His jaw moved up and down like a jackhammer before something strange happened. For a brief moment, Ryan's face turned sweet, as if he was an angel. If you had taken a photo in the split second that he'd swallowed the brownut, you would have sworn he was a nice boy. 'That was pretty good,' he said. I could tell by the tone of his voice that he didn't like admitting it.

'I told you it was good,' said Lin. 'Cindy is in with a real chance of impressing Sir Howard Creame.'

'What's in it?' said Ryan. 'What's in your stupid brownut?'

'A bit of flour, sugar, milk, cocoa, butter… you know…' I didn't like to give *everything* away. Plus, Ryan was paying too much attention for my liking. 'But enough of that. I think Sir Howard Creame will like it. I might even win.'

Ryan growled. 'I'm the only one good enough to win the competition.'

I didn't like the look on his face. He stared at me like he was more interested in taking me down than winning the competition. I remembered the time when he had made a boy who was beating him in a running race fall over. If Ryan Rattle couldn't win himself, he'd always find a way to make sure others failed.

I spent the next few days perfecting the brownut.

Not that it needed perfecting. Everyone who tasted it said it was the best dessert they'd ever had.

Sir Howard Creame would be in town in two days. I was confident I had just the recipe to catch his attention. All I needed to do was buy more ingredients from the supermarket. I decided to wait until the night before the tasting session to head to town for supplies.

That was a bad move.

'There's no flour!' I pointed to an empty space on the shelf.

The teenage boy who worked at Rattle's Grocers scratched his head. 'Let me check the back storeroom.'

'There's no cocoa, either!' I called after him. 'Can you check for that, too?'

I searched the next aisle for sugar, and even that was gone. My empty shopping basket was beginning to feel as light as my head. Something was up.

I ran to the cold section.

Milk. Gone.

Butter. Gone.

What was happening?

The teenage boy found me. 'Excuse me, ma'am –'

'I'm not a ma'am!'

'Oh, sorry, ma'am, some of our stock has been taken off the shelves this week.'

'Taken off the shelves! What do you mean?'

'Sorry, I can't help you, ma'am.'

Surely it was a joke. Rattle's Grocers was usually well stocked. Everything I needed was gone. The ingredients had disappeared like my hopes of winning the competition.

Ryan Rattle stood cross-armed at the exit of his father's supermarket as I left empty-handed. 'I guess you didn't find what you were after,' he said. 'Shame about that.'

Like the pieces of a nightmarish jigsaw puzzle coming together, it dawned on me.

Ryan chuckled to himself.

'It was you!' I said. 'You listened to my ingredients and had them taken off the shelves.'

Ryan put his face close to mine. 'Maybe I did, maybe I didn't,' he said. 'I told you I would win this competition.'

In the space of a few hours, my dreams of impressing Sir Howard Creame had been smashed to pieces, like honeycomb.

I wished Ryan would smash to pieces like honeycomb. I thought about it all the way home but it didn't make me feel any better.

I thumped my fists against the bedroom wall, startling poor Pinko. 'Sorry, little fella,' I said. 'I'm just so mad at that Ryan Rattle. I can't make brownuts without the right ingredients.'

I placed a dead fly in Pinko's web – something I had been doing every day since he arrived. Pinko danced happily and pounced on his meal, spurting out a piece of pink web that drifted out into the night sky.

'You're one cool little guy,' I said. And, briefly, the frustration of the day disappeared.

FIVE

I woke on the morning of Sir Howard Creame's visit to an almost-empty pantry. My brain was just as empty. I couldn't think of anything to make with the few ingredients in our cupboard.

After a quick breakfast, I returned to my room and flopped on my bed. I had to think of something.

'What can I make? What can I make?'

A gentle breeze blew in through my window.

'What can I make? What can I make?'

Something pink and wispy sparkled in the air, floating straight towards me.

'What can I make? What ca–'

Before I had time to react, the pink strand floated into my mouth. I tried to spit it out, but sweetness spread over my tongue; its deliciousness swirled inside my cheeks. The pink strand had taken my tastebuds by storm. It was the most delicious thing I had ever eaten. It made brownuts taste like cardboard in comparison.

Moments later, another pink web floated towards me. I sucked it in. The same sweet taste filled my mouth. It was pure sugary magic.

I walked to my window. I had to find out where the pink strands were coming from.

'Pinko!' I said. 'It's you! *You're* making the strands!'

Pinko jiggled on his web and shot another strand towards me. I swallowed it whole.

I ran to the kitchen and grabbed an empty bowl and fork.

'Do you think you can make more, little fella?' I said. Pinko raced across his web and shot out an enormous strand. I wrapped it around the fork and put it in the bowl. It held together just like the pink fairy floss you buy at the movies.

'I can't lose!' I said.

SIX

Sir Howard Creame arrived at the town hall in a long black limousine. He smiled for some photos with his fans, and signed a few autographs. Everyone was happy to see him.

Once inside the hall, he made his way to a row of tables filled with desserts. The makers of the desserts were standing behind the tables, waiting for Sir Howard Creame to taste their creations.

Lin was in the audience, and she gave me a thumbs-up.

'What's that pitiful bowl of pink gunk?' said Ryan Rattle. He was standing next to me at our table. It was the last one in the hall.

'Spider floss,' I said, without thinking. The name popped into my head and I liked it at once.

'That's one of the dumbest things I've ever heard. Your pink spaghetti doesn't stand a chance against my coconut cake.'

Sir Howard Creame was getting closer to where I was standing. He wasn't giving much away as he worked his way along the row of tables. Every now and then he would write in his notebook and say something like 'not bad' or 'fairly good' or 'well done'.

'I have an advantage standing after you and being last,' said Ryan. 'When he almost vomits trying yours, mine will be even tastier! It will be the final thing he remembers!'

'We'll see,' I said. After everything Ryan had said and done in the past week, I was looking forward to seeing his face when my dessert was tasted. I was as quietly confident as I had ever been about anything. I couldn't get the taste of Pinko's web out of my head.

Sir Howard Creame stepped in front of our table. 'This is rather interesting,' he said.

He picked up a spoon and dipped it into the spider floss.

'Try not to vomit,' said Ryan, quiet enough so only I could hear.

Sir Howard Creame raised the spoon and examined the spider floss. 'So intricately fine,' he said. He put the spoon into his mouth and closed his eyes. He stayed like that for a moment before something strange happened.

He started dancing.

His arms and legs became electric, and he zipped around the hall as though his whole body was on fire.

'Yippee! I have found it!'

The audience clapped and cheered. Lin couldn't contain her excitement and squealed.

Sir Howard Creame caught his breath and returned to my table. 'If you don't mind, I'd like to eat some more.'

He shovelled a great spoonful of spider floss into his mouth and licked his lips. 'I have never tasted anything like it.'

In desperation, Ryan held up a piece of his coconut cake for Sir Howard Creame to try.

'Oh, no, thank you,' said Sir Howard Creame. 'Didn't you read the rules? I'm allergic to coconut.'

Ryan stomped away.

Sir Howard Creame turned to the audience. 'On the last table, in the last town, we have a winner!'

SEVEN

A waiter brings me a huge ice-cream sundae in the shape of the Sydney Opera House. Sir Howard stares intently into my eyes. 'Simply remarkable,' he says. He has been listening the whole time. 'So, that's how you created your spider floss.'

'I brought Pinko along to show you today,' I say. I reach into my pocket and pull out a small plastic container, with pinholes in the lid to allow in air. I unscrew the lid, and Pinko scurries onto my hand.

'Absolutely incredible,' says Sir Howard.

Pinko shoots a strand of pink web into the air, and Sir Howard catches it in his mouth. 'I have dreamed of tasting this again,' he says. He closes his eyes and smacks his lips together.

Pinko shoots out a second strand, and I catch it between my teeth. I wink at my eight-legged friend.

Sir Howard taps the paper on the table in front of me. 'I will most gladly double my offer,' he says. 'I truly mean it. A dessert with this story and taste is worth a lot of money. You will earn your fair share.'

'Thank you very much,' I say. 'But I came here today to tell you some other news.'

Sir Howard's shoulders drop. 'Oh, I see.'

'As much as I would like to share Pinko's recipe with you, I will have to say no.'

Sir Howard looks sad. 'I understand,' he says. 'Something this special needs to be protected.'

'And studied,' I say.

'What do you mean?'

'I'm going to give Pinko to the local entomology society. They can care for him better than I can. And we need to learn about him to give him the best future.'

Pinko jumps up and down at this.

I can't tell if Sir Howard is relieved or even sadder.

He is deep in thought.

'But before I go,' I say, 'there's something I'd like to give you.' I take a folded piece of paper out of my pocket and hand it to Sir Howard.

'What's this?' he says.

'A present for you, for being so kind,' I say.

It's about three months since I visited Sir Howard's famous restaurant. I'm very happy to be back.

Sir Howard insisted Mum and Dad fly first class with me to celebrate the success of his latest dessert.

A waiter takes us to the chef's table. Everyone is staring at us as Sir Howard greets us with warm smiles and handshakes. 'Dear Cindy, how wonderful you could come back. And how delightful to meet your parents.'

'Business seems to be going well,' says Dad. He looks around at the crowded restaurant.

'It's never been better,' says Sir Howard. 'My latest dessert is the most popular yet. It's selling by the thousands.'

'What's it called?' says Mum.

Sir Howard's eyes shine with joy. 'Brownuts,' he says proudly. 'Brownuts.'

●●●○○ EE4 100%

12:43

Saturday 1 July

TANGENTINE TEXTS AGAIN

MESSAGES now

Unknown Number
iMessage
Turn page for more

Turn page to unlock

●●●○○ EE4 12:43 PM 100%

U

Unknown

SUP

Is that you, Tangentine?

Yep.

I changed my phone number.
How did you get the new one?

Guessed it.

I don't believe you.

It's true. Although this time
I didn't guess first go.

How many guesses did it take
you?

Two.

Pfft. You're full of made-up
stories.

That shouldn't surprise you,
Tim. After all, I am fictional.

That's true.

I am always full of surprises.

That's also true.

Did I ever tell you my last name is Blockstock?

That's ridiculous. What a silly name. It can't be true.

Of course it's true, Tim. You just wrote it.

Hmm... I'm not so sure I did.

You just wrote that, too.

I guess so. Then tell me, Tangentine Blockstock, what's your middle name?

Pollywolly.

Tangentine Pollywolly Blockstock. Ha-ha-ha-ha!

What's so funny?

Tangentine Pollywolly Blockstock. Say it aloud.

It does sound rather funny when you say it aloud.

I wonder if the reader just tried saying it aloud...

Probably. If they haven't already, they'd be giving it a go now.

Tangentine Pollywolly Blockstock.

I just remembered something.

What?

You don't have any readers.

Oh yeah, that's right.

'Cause your books are terrible.

Terribly funny.

Awful.

Awfully funny.

Horrible.

Horribly funny.

Not.

Not funny.

Ha-ha-ha-ha! You fell for it.

No, I didn't. I made it up, remember? I set that joke up myself, to have you say it so it would be me who looks funny, and not you. The reader will smile at your joke, which is really my joke.

But you don't have any readers.

I keep forgetting.

You shouldn't forget something like that. You've had no readers since Day One. You should have stuck to lollypop dipping.

Stop insulting me! You're a bit too rude at times. You're an annoying little interruption and I should never have invented you in the first place.

Slow down, Tim. You're getting too defensive. Easy, boy.

Today 1:24pm

Tim?

Hello?

You're not answering.

Did I upset you?

Tim?

Sorry, I'm back. I had to go and check the male.

Don't you mean mail?

No, I had to go and check the man next door.

Huh?

He needed help unpacking the shopping.

Oh.

Yep. I can be a good neighbour at times.

Something doesn't add up.

What doesn't add up.

If you were checking the male, then who was typing my lines:
Tim?
Hello?
You're not answering.
Did I upset you?
Tim?

Gee, I don't know who typed that. How creepy.

I'll say.

Far out. I'm freaked out now. Somebody must have had access to my manuscript.

Who?

I don't know.

Have a think. There must be somebody who inserted those lines. Who could have seen the manuscript?

Maybe it was Sue.

Who's Sue?

The editor of this book.

But that's impossible. She hasn't even read this draft yet.

But it's not a draft. It's a published book, being held right now – by a reader.

You don't have any readers.

I keep forgetting!

So, if Sue didn't add it to the manuscript, then who did?

Maybe the reader imagined it.

YOU DON'T HAVE ANY READERS!

My bad.

#forgetful

#yep

#badwriter

#notsoyep

#trustme

#whyarewehashtagging?

#tomixthingsup

#imokthanks

#huh?

#yousaidsup

#thatwaspartofanentiresentence

#thisisbecomingquitedifficult toread

#itsonlydifficulttoreadbecause yourewritinglongersentences

#youforgotacoupleofapostroph esthere

#youforgottheapostrophesnotme

#howdoesthatwork?

#youtypedmyline

Can we text normally, please? This is becoming ridiculous.

Okay.

Can I ask you something, Tangentine Pollywolly Blockstock?

Sure.

Why did you text me, anyway?

You know why, Tim.

Because you like creating tangents?

Exactly.

You certainly make life interesting.

Finally, you're admitting that I'm valuable.

I guess so.

Thanks, Tim.

But don't forget that golden rule about your Exploding Endings appearances, Tangentine Pollywolly Blockstock.

What's that?

I have the power to end the conversation. Bye.

Hehe.

Have you disappeared?

Perhaps you're being quiet.

Hello?

Tangentine?

Was it me who offended you?

Today 2:53pm

Are you there?

Yeah.

Hehe. I wrote you back in

Maybe it's time to write me out for good.

But the readers would miss you!

HOW MANY TIMES DO I HAVE TO TELL YOU!
YOU DON'T HAVE ANY READERS!!!!!!!!!

Well, if that's the case...
Bye, Tangentine.

Hello?

Are you there?

Tangentine?

Today 3:19pm

I guess you're gone.

What a shame. I really liked having you around.

I mean, you could be a bit annoying at times, but you were fun to write.

Then again, you could be quite rude and you teased me a lot.

It's probably for the best.

Yeah, I'm glad you're gone.

But who am I going to text now? Who will keep me company?

Well, if that's the case...
Bye, Tangentine.

Think, Tim, think.

Maybe I should just write her back in.

But the peace and quiet is so lovely. I could go and do chores. I could put washing on the line. I could go and check the male.

What should I doooooooooo?

Just write me back in.

But I don't think that I should.

Give it a go. It might just work.

I'm not so sure. I don't think it's a good idea.

What could possibly go wrong?

Every time we text each other, things get out of control.

You've got nothing to lose. You might even gain a reader.

Wait a moment... it's you!

Tada!!

Tangentine! You're back!

Thanks to you.

I'm so glad to see you.

Technically, you can't see me.

No?

I'm just words on a screen.

Page.

Page?

Not a screen, this is a book.

It could be an ebook.

Good point.

Did you miss me?

Yep.

Really??

Nope.

Grrrrrr.

I've been thinking, Tangentine Pollywolly Blockstock...

What is it?

I’ve got this big secret and I need to tell someone.

Pick me! Pick me!

Can I trust you?

Absolutely! I won’t tell a soul.

It’s classified information. I haven’t told anyone this before.

You can trust me with your life. Just tell me. What is it?

Okay. I’ll tell you. I’ll tell you my big secret.

I’m listening closely.

I’ve decided to do something special.

Oh! Tell me more! What is it?

I’ve decided to start...

Delivered

Your mobile service advises of the immediate disconnection of this number due to lack of readers.

DEAR READER,
PLEASE EXCUSE ME WHILE I CHANGE MY PHONE NUMBER. I'LL BE BACK ON THE NEXT PAGE.
KIND REGARDS,
TIM HARRIS

INTERPRETING

MRS BLATCHFORD

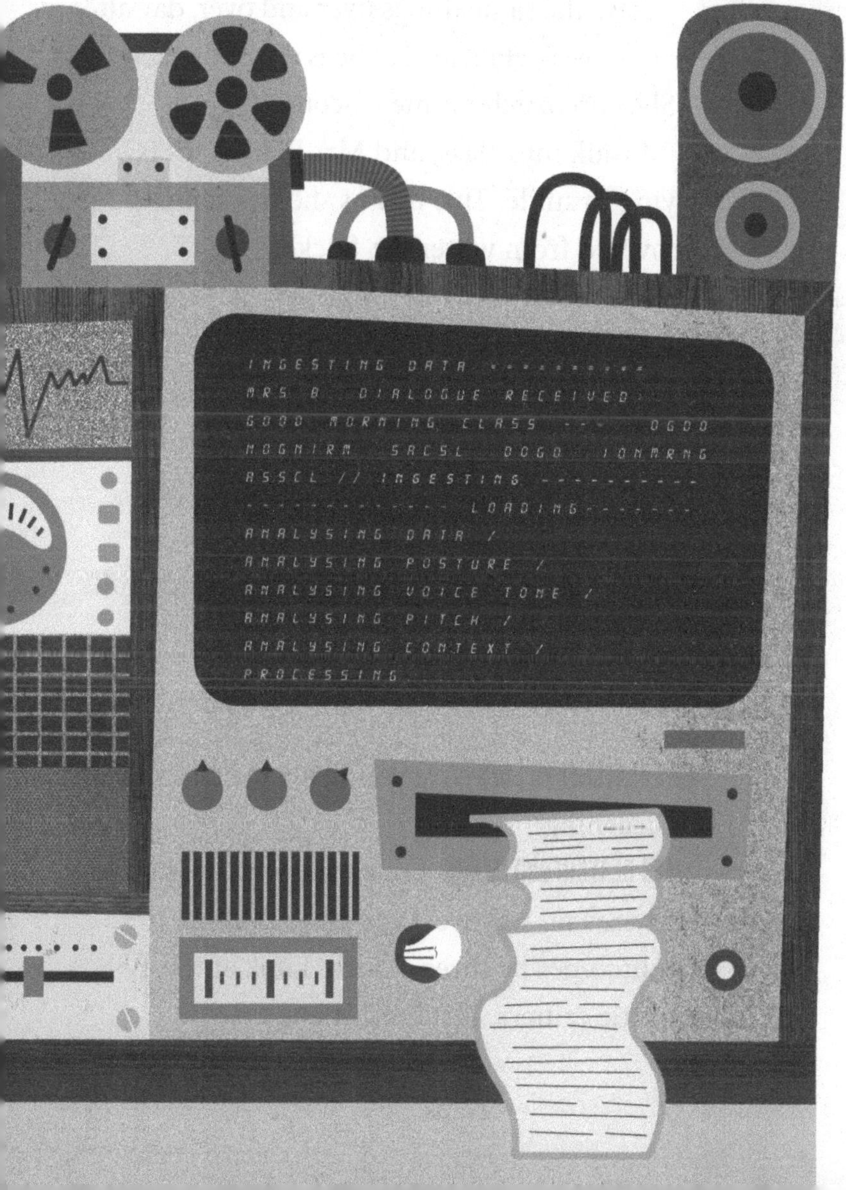

I'm not silly. I know what Mrs Blatchford really means when she says things. She says the same things over and over, day after day, week after week. She is so predictable. She's no match for me – Scotty.

I walk into class, and Mrs Blatchford is trying to smile. This means she has semi-recovered from yesterday. Sucker.

MRS BLATCHFORD SAYS: Good morning, class!
MRS BLATCHFORD MEANS: It's not really a good morning. I hate my job. Only fifty-seven sleeps until the holidays.

MRS BLATCHFORD SAYS: Let's start by marking the roll.
MRS BLATCHFORD MEANS: Let's find out what sort of evil I'll be dealing with today.

MRS BLATCHFORD SAYS: Are you ready for a big day of learning?
MRS BLATCHFORD MEANS: I don't know why I bother. There's no way we'll get through these outcomes by three o'clock. Look at the evil little critters. Just look at 'em.

MRS BLATCHFORD SAYS: Our first lesson is Maths.
MRS BLATCHFORD MEANS: Our first lesson is doomed.

MRS BLATCHFORD SAYS: Who can tell me what a right angle is?
MRS BLATCHFORD MEANS: Shivers! I can't remember what a right angle is. Hopefully, one of the critters will know.

MRS BLATCHFORD SAYS: Scotty, please raise your hand if you would like to share something.
MRS BLATCHFORD MEANS: Scotty, be quiet!

MRS BLATCHFORD SAYS: No, Janelle, a right angle is not the same as an octagonal prism with dots and stripes.
MRS BLATCHFORD MEANS: You're a strange one, Janelle. I wonder what your parents fed you for breakfast this morning.

MRS BLATCHFORD SAYS: Now, who can tell me what a right angle is?
MRS BLATCHFORD MEANS: Please, someone save the lesson.

MRS BLATCHFORD SAYS: Do I need to remind you, Scotty? No calling out.
MRS BLATCHFORD MEANS: Be quiet, Scotty!

MRS BLATCHFORD SAYS: Let's watch an online video about right angles.
MRS BLATCHFORD MEANS: Four years at university, and this is the best I've got.

MRS BLATCHFORD SAYS: Is there someone who would like to press play on the online video?
MRS BLATCHFORD MEANS: There has to be someone in here with a bit of skill.

MRS BLATCHFORD SAYS: Thank you, Victor. Well done.
MRS BLATCHFORD MEANS: Thank goodness for Victor.

MRS BLATCHFORD SAYS: I'll just pause the video here. As you can see, a right angle is made up of ninety degrees. It's shaped like a capital 'L'.
MRS BLATCHFORD MEANS: I'll have to remember that for next time. Who am I kidding? There probably won't be a next time. I want to be an accountant.

MRS BLATCHFORD SAYS: Please stop calling out, Scotty!
MRS BLATCHFORD MEANS: Please stop calling out, Scotty!

MRS BLATCHFORD SAYS: That's the end of the video. I hope you were paying attention.
MRS BLATCHFORD MEANS: That's the end of the video. Sigh.

MRS BLATCHFORD SAYS: Please return to your desks and take out your maths books.
MRS BLATCHFORD MEANS: That should keep the critters occupied for two minutes. I wonder if I have time for another coffee.

MRS BLATCHFORD SAYS: Open up to a new page and rule a margin.
MRS BLATCHFORD MEANS: Find a page without scribble on it and use your ruler to draw something that resembles a straight line.

MRS BLATCHFORD SAYS: Draw a right angle.
MRS BLATCHFORD MEANS: Nail this and it will be the highlight of my career.

MRS BLATCHFORD SAYS: Good try, Lex, but that's an acute angle.

MRS BLATCHFORD MEANS: You clearly weren't watching the video, Lex.

MRS BLATCHFORD SAYS: Good try, Imogen, but that's an obtuse angle.

MRS BLATCHFORD MEANS: You clearly weren't watching the video, Imogen.

MRS BLATCHFORD SAYS: Good try, Scotty, but that's a picture of somebody with seven heads.

MRS BLATCHFORD MEANS: It's not even a very good drawing. Oh well, as long as he's quiet, he can draw whatever he likes.

MRS BLATCHFORD SAYS: Well done, Victor, that's a lovely right angle.

MRS BLATCHFORD MEANS: You really did come from heaven, Victor.

MRS BLATCHFORD SAYS: Please take a look at Victor's book. That is how you draw a right angle.

MRS BLATCHFORD MEANS: Just copy it and I'll pretend I didn't see.

MRS BLATCHFORD SAYS: I said, take a look at Victor's book, not leap out of your chairs and run around.
MRS BLATCHFORD MEANS: Oh dear. I shouldn't have said that.

MRS BLATCHFORD SAYS: Return to your desks at once!
MRS BLATCHFORD MEANS: Order in the house!

MRS BLATCHFORD SAYS: Scotty! Stop rocking the tall bookshelf!
MRS BLATCHFORD MEANS: *Argh*! What a nightmare child!

MRS BLATCHFORD SAYS: The bookshelf is wobbling! Stop it, now!
MRS BLATCHFORD MEANS: Why, why, why didn't I just choose a normal job?

MRS BLATCHFORD SAYS: The bookshelf is falling!
MRS BLATCHFORD MEANS: I hope it lands on top of Scotty!

MRS BLATCHFORD SAYS: Oh!
MRS BLATCHFORD MEANS: Rats! It just missed Scotty's head. What a shame!

MRS BLATCHFORD SAYS: Everyone just calm down and return to your desks.
MRS BLATCHFORD MEANS: What I'd give for a holiday.

MRS BLATCHFORD SAYS: Scotty! Stop chewing on Victor's pencil case.
MRS BLATCHFORD MEANS: *ARRRGH*!!

MRS BLATCHFORD SAYS: That's enough, Scotty! The desk is not a trampoline.
MRS BLATCHFORD MEANS: I can feel my heart aching under the stress. It's too much! I can't take this any more.

MRS BLATCHFORD SAYS: That's it! I've had it up to here, Scotty. To the principal's office.
MRS BLATCHFORD MEANS: That's it! I've had it up to here, Scotty. To the principal's office. And hand in my resignation while you're there!

Mrs Blatchford is so predictable. I know exactly what she means when she says things. I can read her like a book. Even now, sitting outside Principal Sneddon's office, I know exactly what she's saying to him inside.

He's just as easy to pick. Adults are as see-through as cling wrap on a toilet seat.

PRINCIPAL SNEDDON SAYS: Mrs Blatchford, I know this has been a difficult class for you.
PRINCIPAL SNEDDON MEANS: Mrs Blatchford, there's only fifty-seven sleeps until the holidays. Hang in there, lady.

PRINCIPAL SNEDDON SAYS: We would love you to stay on, if you are able.
PRINCIPAL SNEDDON MEANS: Please stay! We can't afford to lose another teacher.

PRINCIPAL SNEDDON SAYS: Yes, I understand Scotty is a very challenging student.
PRINCIPAL SNEDDON MEANS: Hmm. I've got no idea how to control that child.

PRINCIPAL SNEDDON SAYS: I'm sorry to hear that, Mrs Blatchford. Is there nothing I can do to make you stay at the school?
PRINCIPAL SNEDDON MEANS:
Pleeeeeeeeeeeeeeeeeeeeease stay!! We need you here. *I* need you here. We just can't lose another teacher over Scotty.

PRINCIPAL SNEDDON SAYS: Yes, I know, Mrs Blatchford, this reflects poorly on me.

PRINCIPAL SNEDDON MEANS: I give up.

PRINCIPAL SNEDDON SAYS: I'll have a quiet word with Scotty later on.

PRINCIPAL SNEDDON MEANS: What am I going to say to Scotty? My own son is out of control, and nothing I can say or do will fix it.

PRINCIPAL SNEDDON SAYS: Goodbye, Mrs Blatchford.

PRINCIPAL SNEDDON MEANS: Goodbye, Mrs Blatchford. I'm sorry my son and his class got the better of you.

Just as I suspected. Dad was as easy to read as Mrs Blatchford. I wonder who he'll hire next…

SLOW LOTION

ONE

Have you ever wanted something so badly that you were prepared to cheat for it? I have. And so has my twin sister, Charlotte.

Everyone thought Charlotte was the best choice for school captain. She always scored well in tests, won running races and volunteered for jobs. But I knew I could handle the role of school captain just as well as she could. I was sick of people overlooking me because I always came second to my sister.

It all started on our eleventh birthday. Charlotte and I were given gift vouchers for Barb's Beauty Shop. First chance we got, we visited the store; we couldn't wait to see what we could get. We took Em along. She's our best friend.

'There are so many creams here,' said Charlotte. She stood in front of a huge shelf dedicated to pimple cream.

'Freakin' chicken,' said Em, holding up a thin plastic bottle. 'This oil makes your nose grow longer.'

I picked up a small container with 'Slow Lotion' written on the side.

'Hmm,' I said. 'Apparently, this one helps you to slow down and relax. I could use some of that for the school-captain selections.'

Charlotte's ears must have pricked up at the words 'school captain' because she scooted over. 'What is it?

What do you have?'

'Slow Lotion,' I replied. 'It says it's good for clear thinking and stress release.'

Charlotte must have been thinking what I was thinking. 'I need some of that!' she announced.

'You'll be disappointed,' said Em. 'Ali has the last jar.'

Charlotte's face dropped, and I knew this was my chance. It was my opportunity to get an edge over my sister. For eleven years, she had been beating me. It was time for the tide to turn. I took the Slow Lotion to the counter.

'Freakin' chicken! This cream removes freckles.' Em chuckled to herself and wandered off to check out some other shelves.

Charlotte hastily rummaged through some bottles in a discount bin – no doubt searching for more Slow Lotion.

I had just finished paying when Charlotte marched to the counter. She had a determined look in her eye. It was the same look she had every time she beat me.

'Don't be too confident, Ali,' she said. 'I found something that will help me become captain, for sure!'

I gulped. 'What is it?'

'You'll see,' she said triumphantly. 'Just you wait.'

TWO

The selections for school captain were approaching, and everyone at school was talking about it.

'Leon will be boy captain,' said Em. 'Everyone knows it.'

'Yep,' I said. 'For sure.'

'And everyone knows I will be girl captain,' said Charlotte. 'There's only room for one twin at the top.'

The school principal, Mr Bosworth, called the students together and spoke to them about the appointment process.

'This year, we have decided to try something different,' he said. 'We have some excellent candidates and we want to make the selection process as fair as possible.'

Em rubbed some cream into her face as she listened.

Mr Bosworth continued. 'We are holding a series of tests to let our candidates show what they're made of.'

I watched as everyone listened closely. I didn't like tests at the best of times. My knees began to tremble. I shot a glance at Charlotte who was looking as confident as ever.

'Starting from now, we will hold one test each week for the next four weeks. The candidates who best excel – one boy and one girl – will be appointed school captains for next year.'

My knees knocked even harder. I hated pressure like this. It was a good thing I had Slow Lotion handy.

'I am thrilled to tell you that the first test is to be held straightaway. It is to be a test of organisational skills. As you know, captains are expected to deliver notes to each classroom in the school. This race is to see who can sort notes into class groups and deliver them on time.

'Perfect,' whispered Charlotte, smiling to herself.

The students piled out onto the school oval, and Mr Bosworth invited all the candidates to line up at one end. I was surprised to see Em join the row of girl candidates. Mr Bosworth seemed to make a big point of including her.

The boys were first. It was a chance for me to catch my breath. I was so nervous.

'Leon will flog the others,' said Charlotte. 'Just like

I'll flog you.'

I had never beaten Charlotte in any sort of running race before. I didn't like my chances. Perhaps I could sort the notes faster. That was my only hope.

As expected, Leon won the boys' race. He sorted and delivered the notes in no time. Second place was a long way behind.

It was time for the girls to race. My heart was pounding like a drum. It was time to use some Slow Lotion. I needed to relax.

I pulled the jar from my pocket and unscrewed the lid. The lotion looked like sunscreen, though it smelt like strawberries. I scooped out a large blob and rubbed it into my legs to stop them from shaking.

A warm feeling spread up my legs and through my body. My heart slowed to a steady pace and my thinking became clear. A map of the school appeared in my mind, and I knew the fastest route to deliver the notes.

Mr Bosworth handed Em her pile of notes. 'I'm so pleased you're included. Here are your blue notes.'

He handed a pile of red notes to Charlotte without saying a word. Then he gave me some green notes.

'This should be a piece of cake,' said Charlotte. She bent down and rubbed something into her legs, just as I had done.

Mr Bosworth blew his whistle, and the girl candidates started sorting their notes into piles. It was very even.

Soon, the girls took off in different directions around the school. All of them except me, that is. My legs felt like they were glued to the ground. I had to check to see if they were even moving. They were, though barely. I was running in slow motion. The strange thing was, I felt as alert as ever. I knew the quickest way around the school. The only problem was it would take me forever to do it.

I had only taken a few steps when people began cheering. Charlotte had won.

'Congratulations, Leon and Charlotte,' said Mr Bosworth. 'You are the winners of the first test. Special mention goes to Charlotte. I've never seen anyone run so fast!'

Everyone clapped. I frowned. I hated Charlotte beating me.

'What on earth did you rub into your legs?' I asked.

'I'll show you when I'm school captain,' said Charlotte. 'Until then, you don't need to worry about it.'

'I'm just happy to be appointed as a candidate,' said Em. 'Ever since your birthday, people have been including me in things. It's freakin' awesome.'

I kept the jar of Slow Lotion in a safe place until the following test, hopeful it would help me. As it turned out, it ended up being *exactly* what I needed.

THREE

Mr Bosworth stood at the front of the hall.

'This week's test is a writing challenge,' he said. 'Our future captains must be able to write intelligent articles to go in the school's newsletter. You have thirty minutes to write a sample.'

I fidgeted as I waited for the paper to be handed out. My mind raced with ideas, though I couldn't pin one down. Nerves were becoming a problem again.

I knew the Slow Lotion would help me relax, so I pulled the jar from my pocket and massaged some into my temple. It worked. My thoughts slowed and the ideas started organising themselves in my mind.

I glanced at Charlotte, just in time to see her rub something into her hands.

'Freakin' chicken,' whispered Em. 'This is a bit exciting.'

Mr Bosworth tapped a bell, and the candidates started writing.

My mind, now completely relaxed and free from distraction, began to weave some clever ideas together. Everything made perfect sense, and the article flowed onto the paper like a river of golden thoughts. My page was filled when Mr Bosworth tapped the bell thirty minutes later.

I looked across at Charlotte. She had written eight pages, and her hand was shaking uncontrollably.

Em was eager to talk about it at lunchtime.

'I don't like writing,' she said. 'But it's freakin' brilliant to be included in everything.'

'I think I did really well,' I replied. 'I wrote a full page.'

'I wrote eight pages,' said Charlotte, trying to stop her hand from shaking. 'It was too easy.'

Mr Bosworth called the students together at the end of lunch to announce the winners.

'Congratulations, Leon,' he said. 'I enjoyed your article about the need for more water fountains.'

Everyone applauded. Charlotte clapped as though her hands were on fire.

'The girls wrote some… *interesting* articles,' said Mr Bosworth. 'However, the choice was very easy in the end. Congratulations, Ali. I've never read such a knowledgeable article about the importance of diversity in creating strong community.'

'Whaty-whaty?' said Em.

Mr Bosworth handed Charlotte her essay. 'You need to work on your handwriting,' he said. 'I couldn't read a single word on any of the eight pages. I think you need to slow down.'

Charlotte slinked away. Her advantage had just been lost. We were even.

I lay in bed that night thinking about Slow Lotion. It seemed to affect the part of my body I rubbed it into. It had slowed down my legs in the delivery race, cleared my thoughts in the writing and, overall, helped me relax. I knew if I used it just right, it could help me win the remaining tests.

I wondered about Charlotte. Whatever she was using was having some weird effects, too. She smashed the note-delivery race, then followed it up with eight pages of sloppy work. She was very inconsistent.

My final thought turned to the next test. I wondered what Mr Bosworth had up his sleeve.

FOUR

'This week's test involves a lot of hard work,' said Mr Bosworth. 'You are to practise preparing the hall for assembly. You need to demonstrate how to put the chairs out, tie the curtains back and set up the sound system. As you all know, assembly set-up is rushed, as our dancers use the hall each lunch.'

The boys went first. They had to take it in turns while Mr Bosworth timed them. Leon worked his way through the giant school hall as expected – quickly and efficiently. He unstacked chairs, laid them out, dashed to the sound system and turned it on, tied back the curtains and even stopped to make Mr Bosworth a cup of tea from the kitchenette near the back. He won easily.

The girls were next. I rubbed Slow Lotion into my temple, wanting to have clear thoughts about the job. I couldn't risk rubbing it into my arms or legs as that might slow me down. Most of all, I wanted to calm my nerves. They were driving me nuts.

'Freakin' chicken, this is a hard test,' said Em. She put a small container in her pocket.

'Tell me about it,' I said. 'I don't know how I'll beat Charlotte in this one.'

I studied Charlotte. She was rubbing something into her arms and legs and appeared as confident as ever. I remembered the first physical challenge and how Mr Bosworth raved about her speed.

Mr Bosworth asked Em to go first.

She was steady as she moved around the hall, though she accidentally knocked over two chairs.

'Freakin' chicken!'

I waited for a few other girls to have their turn before it was mine.

I went about my business in logical order, starting with the technology. I connected the microphone lines with ease, my relaxed state of mind making sure of it. I followed it up by pulling the stage curtains back and securing them with a difficult sailor's knot I had once learned. The chairs were my final job and, although it took a long time to line them up, the hall was soon in working order.

'Thank you, Ali,' said Mr Bosworth. He turned to Charlotte. 'After the boys have put everything away again, it's your turn.'

Charlotte's arms and legs twitched as she waited. She poked her tongue out at me. 'You have no hope,

Ali. I've got you covered.'

'When you're ready,' said Mr Bosworth.

Charlotte raced to the stack of chairs in a split second. She zipped back and forth, between the rows and stacks of chairs, like a cheetah. I couldn't believe my eyes.

Before I knew what was happening, she was onto the curtain and sound system. She was finished in a flash.

'Very impressive,' said Mr Bosworth. 'What an amazing effort; just what's required after the dancers clear out at the end of lunch.'

Em opened up a packet of chips and took a deep sniff. 'Chicken flavour,' she said. 'Freakin' chicken awesomeness.'

'Charlotte blitzed that challenge,' I said. 'I've never seen anyone move so fast.'

Em turned to my twin. 'How did you do it so quickly?'

'Just a little trick I know,' said Charlotte. She tapped a small bulge in her pocket.

'I knew it!' I said. 'I knew you were cheating!'

'And you're not?' said Charlotte. 'I know you've been using that Slow Lotion or whatever it is you bought at Barb's Beauty Shop. You can't fool me. If you can do it, so can I.'

I could feel my face become hot. 'I'm sick of losing to you all the time. I deserve a chance to be captain just as much as you.'

'Freakin' calm down,' said Em. 'You're family, remember?' She took out a small container of cream and rubbed some into her face.

'I guess so,' I said. Though I wanted more than ever to beat Charlotte.

FIVE

The students and teachers crammed the hall the following week. The final challenge was to be a public-speaking competition. Each of the candidates had to explain why they should be appointed school captain. There was only one catch: you were given just one minute to make your point.

The boys spoke first. Leon was amazing. His speech

was flawless. Everybody loved what he had to say.

I took a deep breath. The girls were next. It was make-or-break time. I had one last chance to prove I was good enough to be captain.

Mr Bosworth asked Charlotte to speak first. I saw her rub something into her lips as she stepped up to the microphone.

Before I knew it, Charlotte's mouth started moving in ways unknown to humankind. It opened and closed at lightning speed. It flashed and gnashed and spattered and chatted. Nobody could understand what she was saying. She sounded like a chipmunk in fast-forward mode. Her speech was over in seconds.

Mr Bosworth was rattled. 'Thank you for that… *attempt*, Charlotte,' he said. 'Perhaps you could work at *slowing* down.'

Charlotte's face fell. She knew she had blown it.

The word 'slowing' echoed in my anxious mind. It was as though Mr Bosworth had said it just for me. I rubbed a large dollop of Slow Lotion around my lips and stroked some into my temple for good measure. I felt calmer right away. Though my lips felt heavy.

Em spoke next and challenged the students to buy more chicken-flavoured chips. 'They're awesome!' she concluded.

Everyone giggled, and Em walked back to her seat.

A few more girls spoke before Mr Bosworth invited me to the microphone. I was the last speaker. It was time to move out of Charlotte's shadow and show the world who Ali truly was. It was time to be the more brilliant twin. This minute was mine to own.

'Gooooooooooood afternoooooooooooon, Mr Boooooooswooooooooooorrth, staaaaaaaaaaff and stuuuuuuuuuuuuudents,' I said. My lips flopped around in slow motion like a cow chewing grass. I couldn't control their speed. 'I wooooooooooooooould liiiiiiiiiiiiiiiike tooooooo oooooooooooooooooooooooooooooooooooo –'

Mr Bosworth snatched the microphone from me. 'Er… that was… um… thank you, Ali.'

A couple of students clapped out of politeness. I was so embarrassed.

I returned to my seat next to Charlotte, praying it was some kind of slow nightmare and I would wake up in real time.

Mr Bosworth awarded the best speech to Dolly, a quiet girl in my class.

'It's in the bag,' whispered Charlotte, whose lips had returned to their normal speed. 'Two to one in the challenges. You and Dolly don't stand a chance.'

'It's been an exciting four weeks,' said Mr Bosworth. 'The candidates have all worked hard to prove themselves.'

All eyes were now on the principal. 'I would like to announce the boy captain first. Please give a big round of applause to Leon. He was superior in each of the tests and will make a splendid school captain.'

Leon walked to the stage and shook Mr Bosworth's hand.

'That was predictable,' said Charlotte. 'Just like the fact he's about to appoint me.' She unzipped a pocket on her dress. 'I told you I'd tell you my secret when I was chosen as captain.' She handed me a small jar of

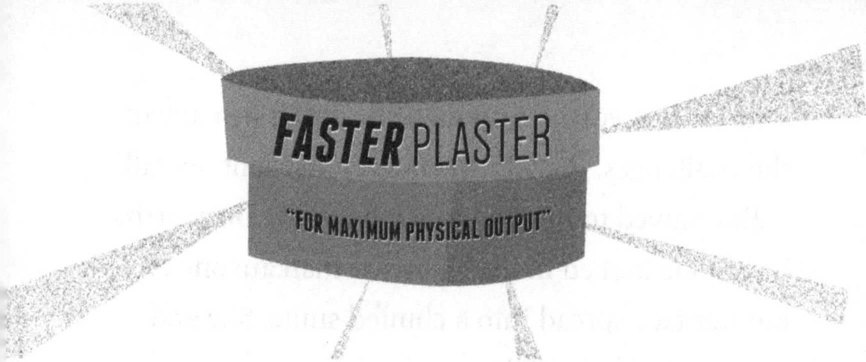

cream. 'This beats Slow Lotion, any day.'

Faster Plaster was written on the label. Underneath was a description: *For maximum physical output.*

'And now it's time to appoint the girl captain,' said Mr Bosworth. 'It has been a very interesting competition.'

Everyone stared at Charlotte. She was leading the challenges and was bound to be selected. She had a big grin on her face.

'There can only be one winner,' said Mr Bosworth. 'Please give a round of applause for your newly appointed girl captain – Em!'

A hush swept over the entire hall. Shock was in the air.

'Freakin' chicken,' said Em.

'Frrrreeeeeeeeeeakiiiiiiiing chiiiiiiiiiiicken indeeeeeeeeeeeeeeeeeeeeeeed,' I said. The Slow Lotion still hadn't worn off.

'The decision to appoint Em was easy in the end,'

said Mr Bosworth. 'Although she didn't win any of the challenges, she was the most consistent overall.'

Em moved to the stage and shook Mr Bosworth's hand. She looked more surprised than anyone else, but her face spread into a chuffed smile. She and Leon would be captains.

Em gave the other girl candidates a hug. She pulled a small container from her pocket, undid the lid, and rubbed some cream onto her cheeks.

'What's that?' said Charlotte, leaning over to inspect.

'Just some stuff I bought at Barb's Beauty Shop,' said Em. 'I have no idea what it is, but it feels nice on my skin.'

'Whaaaaaaaaaaat iiiiiiissssssss iiiiiiiit caaaaaaaaaallllllllllled?' I asked.

'Appointment Ointment,' she replied. 'Whatever the freakin' chicken *that* means.'

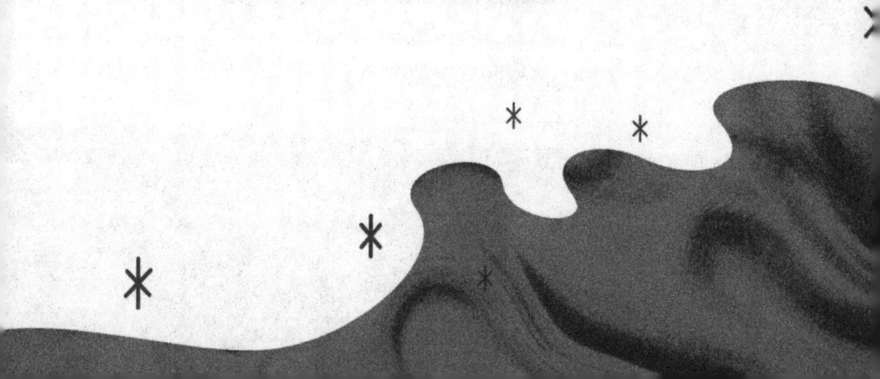

Page Wars
Part 1
Starring:
Left Page as 'Lefty'
Right Page as 'Righty'
Baby Page as 'Baby Page'

IT IS A WELL-KNOWN FACT THAT THE LEFT PAGE IS FAR GREATER THAN THE RIGHT PAGE. THE LEFT PAGE IS, AND WILL ALWAYS BE, THE SUPERIOR SIDE OF A BOOK.

WELL, WELL, WELL... IT SEEMS BABY PAGE HAS BEEN VOTED TO YOU, LEFTY.

WHAT HAVE I BEEN SAYING ALL ALONG, RIGHTY? THE READERS LOVE ME. NO WONDER THEY VOTED BABY PAGE TO THIS SIDE.

IT DOESN'T MATTER. I KNOW SOMETHING YOU DON'T KNOW.

YOU COULDN'T POSSIBLY HAVE ANY MORE TRICKS UP YOUR SLEEVE.

I DON'T HAVE TO WORRY ABOUT TRICKS. YOU HAVE CAUSED THIS PROBLEM FOR YOURSELF.

WHAT PROBLEM? WHAT ARE YOU TALKING ABOUT, RIGHTY?

YOU'LL SEE.

YOU OBVIOUSLY DON'T KNOW
ANYTHING ABOUT BABIES.

TOLD. YOU. SO.

I'LL SORT
THIS NOISE OUT;
JUST YOU WAIT!

WE'LL SEE...

HA-HA! LOOK WHO HAS COME OUT ON TOP – AGAIN! I AM ALWAYS IN COMPLETE CONTROL.

JUST YOU WAIT - THINGS ARE ABOUT TO GO DOWNHILL FOR YOU, LEFTY.

WANNA BUY THIS FOR FIVE BUCKS?

ONE

I wouldn't call it stealing. It's just that I needed the money. Three thousand dollars, actually. Borrowing would be more accurate. Yeah, I borrowed three thousand dollars.

The whole thing started when I saw an ad on television for a luxury holiday in Fiji.

Mum's eyes became dreamy. 'That would be nice,' she said. 'I wish I had a spare three thousand dollars.'

Mum only ever became dreamy like that whenever she wanted something. She did it all the time when

she visited the second-hand shop. She was always coming home with bits and pieces.

'Me, too,' said Jet. Jet was only seven and always agreed with whatever Mum and I said. It was so annoying. 'I wish I had three thousand dollars to go there, too.'

I stared at the television. Smiling holiday-makers ate ice cream by the pool. They rode jetskis and snorkelled. The Fijian sun beat down on their arms. They were happy and relaxed, being waited on like members of the Royal Family. I wanted that life. I wanted to go to Fiji and live the high life by the pool. I needed three thousand dollars.

Mum sighed. 'It'll be back to the caravan park for us this Christmas.'

'Back to the caravan park,' repeated Jet dimly.

Not me. I wasn't going back to the caravan park where the only people having a good time were the flies and mosquitoes. Flies and mosquitoes aren't people, by the way. They're insects. And I don't like insects. I don't like the caravan park. I like Fiji.

I choofed off to my room to start planning. I had to think of a money-making idea.

Perhaps I could learn an instrument and busk.

Nah, too time-consuming.

Maybe I could do chores for Mum.

Nah, she's too stingy for that type of thing.

I could get a proper job.

No way. Just no. Too responsible. Plus, I think you have to be fourteen or something.

I could make something and sell it.

Yeah, that sounds doable!

What could I make? There wasn't much in my room to give me any ideas, so I opened my desk drawer. I found a few pieces of green cardboard and some white paper I had borrowed from school. That would have to do.

What would people want that could be made with

paper and cardboard? My phone beeped. I glanced at the screen.

Of course! Screenshots! Everybody loves taking screenshots on their phones. A screenshot on cardboard would save them from looking at their actual phones all the time. Think of the battery power they could save!

I copied the home screen of my phone on the white paper. It took almost ten minutes to draw because I had to get the app icons just right. The next screenshot only took five minutes because I was much better at it by then. The last two screenshots took about a minute each because I was getting really, really good at it.

There were four screenshots in all. They were just like the home screen on my phone. I glued each one on its own piece of green cardboard.

Working out the price was the hard part. I needed three thousand dollars to go to Fiji. Three thousand dollars divided by four was seven hundred and fifty dollars. That was too much for a screenshot.

I settled on five bucks.

I wrote the price on each one and put them back in the drawer. The next day after school, I would be ready to start my money-making mission.

TWO

We lived in a busy street. There were always people walking past our house. Those people were now my customers.

'Wanna buy this for five bucks?'

The lady ignored me as she walked past with her dog. That was rude. You should never ignore people. I bet they don't ignore you in Fiji.

I plonked myself on the grass in our front yard and waited for the next person to pass by. With Mum still at work and Jet watching television, I could sell screenshots without being caught.

'Wanna buy this for five bucks?'

A man with a kind face stopped. 'What are you selling?'

'I made this screenshot of a phone. Here.' I handed him the cardboard screenshot.

'It's a very fine piece of work,' he said.

'Would you like to buy it?' I asked.

The man had understanding eyes. He looked at the screenshot and then back at me. I could tell he was remembering something.

'When I was your age,' he said, 'I used to sell lemonade at the front of my house.'

I grinned. The man understood me.

'I'll buy it.' He smiled.

'Thank you,' I said.

The man gave me five dollars and walked away, whistling to himself as he gazed at the cardboard screenshot. What a nice guy. Maybe he was from Fiji.

With five dollars in my pocket, I felt like the king of the world. I felt like I could sell a thousand cardboard screenshots.

I couldn't have been more wrong.

I didn't sell another screenshot that day. Not one. I didn't sell another screenshot the next day. Zero. Or the next. Zilch. Lack of sales was a problem.

Maybe the screenshot idea wasn't so great, after all.

I needed to come up with a new idea.

THREE

'Wanna buy these for five bucks?'

Mum wouldn't miss a few knives and forks.

A lady wearing a striped jumper stopped to check out the cutlery. 'Only five dollars?

She sounded doubtful.

'Five bucks,' I confirmed.

'What a bargain,' she said. 'I'll take them.'

She paid the five dollars and walked away, clearly happy with her bargain buy.

I snuck back inside to clean out more of the cutlery drawer. Twenty-six more pieces of cutlery for five dollars was a fair deal.

I sold them to the very next person who walked past our house.

'Are we missing some cutlery?' Mum asked that night.

'I don't think so,' I said. 'Have you checked the dishwasher?'

'Yeah, but there are mostly spoons in it,' she replied. 'I was sure we had more knives and forks.'

I shrugged.

'Oh, well,' she said. 'I'll pick up some more at the second-hand store tomorrow.' Her face went dreamy.

I remained tight-lipped, though, once we sat at the dinner table, I tried to distract her.

'Spoons have many uses,' I said. 'You can do a lot with a spoon.'

'We don't need any more spoons. I just don't understand where the knives and forks could have gone.'

'I'm sure they'll turn up,' I said. 'At least we can eat with the spoons.'

Baffled, Jet picked up his spoon and poked at his roast pork.

'You can cut with a spoon,' I said. 'All you have to do is turn it on its side, and *bam* – knife!'

'I just don't understand…' said Mum.

'Spoons can stab,' I said brightly. 'You just have to push harder, and *bam* – fork!'

Mum sighed and attempted to cut the pork with the side of her spoon.

'The best part about spoons,' I grinned, 'is that they can be spoons. Pick up a spoon, and *bam* – spoon! All you need is spoons.'

The rest of dinner was uneventful.

Afterwards, I retreated to my room to count the cash while Mum rummaged around the kitchen searching for any more signs of cutlery life.

I added the day's earnings to my screenshot money. While a couple of cutlery sales were good progress, they were nothing compared to what would happen the next day.

FOUR

I'm a clever kid. I like to work in systems.

The utensil drawer was underneath the cutlery

drawer. That was my next target.

A lady who kept looking at her phone bought the tongs, potato masher and wooden spoon. It was a quick sale. Though I should have asked her if she needed a screenshot, too.

Next, I sold the spatula, rolling pin and cheese grater to one of our neighbours.

The balloon whisk, digital timer and ladle followed. I was on a roll!

Then I sold the cake server, ice-cream scoop and plastic juicer.

Four sales and twenty bucks later, I was back in the kitchen, working my way through the drawers and cupboards. Mum hardly used any of that stuff. She wouldn't miss it.

I sold the sandwich maker to a mother and her baby, and rushed back inside for more.

Mum arrived home carrying a box filled with cutlery and kitchen utensils. I couldn't

believe my luck!

'I went to the second-hand shop today,' she said. 'I thought I'd top up our supplies.'

'Good move, Mum,' I said.

She hurried to the kitchen and started emptying the box into the drawers. She was too excited to notice the missing bits and pieces.

After dinner, Mum clanged around in the kitchen, muttering to herself about the need to buy more second-hand things. 'I can't remember where I put the sandwich maker,' I heard her say.

While Mum pottered in the kitchen, Jet and I pottered in front of the television, eating ice cream.

'You can do a lot with a spoon,' I reminded Jet.

The ad for the Fijian holiday flashed on the screen, and I stopped thinking about spoons.

'Book now for a once-in-a-lifetime chance to relax in Fiji.'

The same happy faces of holiday-makers filled the screen. My whole body tingled. My mission in life was as clear as Fiji's coral waters. A tropical holiday was my destiny.

'Book tomorrow to receive free use of a jetski. We'll even include unlimited soft drinks, delivered to your room.'

'I could do with unlimited soft drinks!' I said.

'What?' said Jet.

'Nothing,' I said. I couldn't risk having Jet on my case. He smiled at his spoon and shovelled in another mouthful of ice cream.

I lay awake in bed that night for hours, dreaming of riding a jetski in a giant pool of soft drink. It really was a once-in-a-lifetime opportunity. I couldn't miss out on the chance. The only problem was that I had to book the next day. So, after lots of thinking, I came to realise there was only one thing to do.

FIVE

Carrying a fifty-inch flat screen television is not an easy task. But I got it out to the front yard in the end. You can do a lot of surprising things when you want to go to Fiji and get awesome upgrades.

Mum was at work and Jet was at soccer training, so it was the perfect time to strike. The television was sure to go quickly.

I saw a teenage boy on a bike.

'Wanna buy this for five bucks?'

The boy stopped pedalling and eyed me suspiciously. 'Five bucks. Are you serious?'

I nodded. 'Call your friends,' I said. 'There's about to be a sale of serious proportion. Right here. In five minutes.'

The teenager's eyes widened. 'Cool. I'll make a few calls.'

He gave me five dollars and promised to return to collect the television with some of his friends.

Sure enough, a few minutes later, right on cue,

I opened the front door to let in a bunch of excited teens.

'Everything is five bucks!' I announced. 'Just leave the spoons and beds.'

My Fijian upgrade was just hours away. The sale had started.

The teenagers called more of their friends. Word quickly spread, and soon loads and loads of people who were searching for bargains swarmed the house.

Lounge – sold!

Shampoo – sold!

Dining table – sold!

Fridge – sold!

Computer – sold!

Grandma's antique piano – sold! And at a bargain price, I might add.

Socks – sold!

Coat hangers – sold!

Oven – sold!

Spoons – please put them down.

Office desk – sold!

Filing cabinet – sold!

Everything sold.

Everything.

Everything except the spoons and beds. After all, we had to sleep somewhere and spoons have many uses.

The crowd left, arms filled with our old stuff. My pockets were filled with cash.

I rushed to my room to count the money.

Three thousand dollars. Perfect.

It was time to book a holiday. It was time to go to Fiji.

SIX

A waiter walks over to me and takes my empty glass.

'Another soft drink, sir?'

'Yes, please,' I say.

I lie by the pool, living the life of a royal, the Fijian sun beating down on my arms.

I'll call Mum tomorrow. I'll tell her the truth. I'll tell her how I borrowed a few of our things and sold them. I'll tell her how the booking price only included a one-way ticket. I'll tell her that I'm stuck in Fiji.

I take a sip of the soft drink – my sixteenth, I think – and lie back on the chair. It shouldn't be too hard to get back to Australia. Not when you're as clever as me.

I lean over to the honeymooners sitting next to me. 'Excuse me,' I say, pointing to the chair I'm relaxing on. 'Wanna buy this for five bucks?'

●●●○○ EE4 100%

5:32

Saturday 1 July

TANGENTINE TEXTS FOR A FAVOUR

MESSAGES now

Unknown Number
iMessage
Turn page for more

Turn page to unlock

●●●○○ EE4 5:32 PM 100%

Unknown

Today 5:32pm

SUP

Please, please tell me this is not who I think it is?

Who do you think it is?

You know who.

Just say my name.

I can't stand the thought of it.

Come on. Just say it. You know you want to.

I don't want to.

Just say it!

sigh If it will keep you off my back... Hello, Tangentine.

Yay! You said my name.

And I regret it already.

No, you don't. You just think you do.

Oh, I do. Trust me!

You really don't.

How did you even get my number? I changed it on page 55. Surely you didn't guess it again.

Yes, indeed. The guessing queen strikes again.

It's gotta be mathematically impossible. The chances must be a million to one.

I'm one in a million.

A million times annoying.

This conversation is really going nowhere.

I'm planning on keeping it that way.

Come on, Tim. You're supposed to be the funny guy. Where's your enthusiasm? Where's your spark?

The only spark I want is the one that zaps you out of here.

He-he. I see what you did there.

What do you want, Tangentine Pollywolly Blockstock? Is there a reason you texted me?

Well, now that you mention it, I need a favour.

A favour? You?

Yep.

You've never asked for a favour before.

There's a first for everything.

I'm not sure about this. What will the readers think?

You don't have any readers!

I keep forgetting about that. Sorry.

It's just one tiny favour.

What's in it for me?

You shouldn't do favours and expect something in return.

That's for me to decide.

Do you want to hear what the favour is or not?

I guess so.

I need fifty bucks.

Fifty bucks! What for?

It's a secret.

I need to know.

But it's a secret.

You have to tell me.

Why?

Because I'm the one lending you the money. You need to tell me out of courtesy.

I'm sorry. I can't do that.

Then forget about it. I'm not lending you fifty bucks if you're not going to have the decency to tell me what you need it for.

Please, Tim, I really need the money.

Yeah, and I'm supposed to believe that.

sniffs
:(

shakes head

crying
nobody loves me

shakes head

upset
betrayed

I can tell you're not going to give up. Will you leave me alone if I lend you fifty bucks?

You know I can't promise that, Tim. I like texting you.

I just can't win. Okay. I'll do it. I'll lend you fifty bucks.

You're the best!

How should I get the money to you?

Bank transfer, please.

Okay, send through your details, and I'll transfer the money now.

I don't like giving out my details over the phone. You should have remembered that from Exploding Endings: *Dingbats & Lollypop Arms*.

Then how are you going to give me your bank details?

Try guessing the bank details. It's how I got your phone number three times across two books. It's really not as hard as people think it is.

Ha! You must be out of your mind.

You'd be surprised what you can do when you put your mind to it.

I'd like to put my mind to erasing you. But I think I've committed to lending you fifty bucks.

Just trust me on this, Tim. Concentrate really hard, log on to your internet banking and guess my details. I'll tell you if it works.

You stress me out. Okay, I'll give it a go. I just have to open up the bank app.

Any luck?

It worked!

Really?

Yep. I'll show you the receipt.

EE NATIONAL BANK

NOTIFICATION OF TRANSFER

Amount: $50.00

Receipt Number: EENB 5142764894987

From: Tim Harris / 22816592

To: Tangentine P. Blockstock / 31599801

Date: 01 July 2020

Time: 6:03PM (AEST)

I don't believe it!

I told you it would work. Guessing is underrated.

I'm shocked.

Don't be.

If you say so.

I like you, Tim.

Make up your mind. One day you like me, the next day you don't.

Today I do.

Can you show this affection by leaving me alone?

You know I can't do that. I'm addicted to texting you.

Can you be addicted to leaving me alone?

It's never going to happen, Tim. You should know that by now.

So, why are you hanging around? I loaned you the fifty bucks. The favour is done. Isn't it time to go?

Not really. I need to ask you something.

What?

I need another favour.

Another favour? What for? What else could you possibly need?

I need another fifty bucks.

But I just loaned you fifty bucks. What do you need another fifty bucks for?

It's a secret.

You and your secrets. This is becoming ridiculous.

Please, Tim. I really need your help. Be kind to your favourite character.

You're not my favourite character.

Who is your favourite character?

My readers.

They're not characters. Plus, you don't have any!

Man, I keep forgetting! Stop annoying me, you pain!

That's not very nice.

Whatever.

Please, please, please just loan me fifty more bucks.

Why should I?

Because I need your help.

thinking about it

I promise I won't borrow any more money from you. This is the last fifty bucks I need.

Okay. I'll do it. I hope I'm doing the right thing.

Yay! Thank you!

I'll log back on to the bank app.

Did the money come through?

It did!

EE NATIONAL BANK

NOTIFICATION OF TRANSFER

Amount: $50.00

Receipt Number: EENB 5142764894988

From: Tim Harris / 22816592

To: Tangentine P. Blockstock / 31599801

Date: 01 July 2020

Time: 6:12PM (AEST)

Glad it arrived. Now, will you leave me alone?

Um... there's one last thing I need to ask.

You've got to be kidding me. What is it?

I received a letter from the Australian Agency for Fictional Characters.

And?

They said that you owe me character royalties.

This is all news to me.

You owe me a hundred bucks.

No, I don't!

Yes, you do. You have been using me in your stories and you owe me financial compensation. The going rate for book characters is a hundred bucks.

This is an outrage.

You should have thought about it before you wrote me into your books.

I demand to see proof!

Here's a photo of their letter.

Okay.

Dear Tangentine,

This letter is to inform you of your right to book-character royalties.

Tim Harris owes you the sum of $100.00.

If this amount is not paid within two weeks, please notify us and we will take legal action.

Kind regards,
Australian Agency for Fictional Characters

:)

How am I supposed to pay you?

They recommend bank transfer.

Hang on. Let me log back on to the bank app…

This is crazy…

Oh, no! I have no more money in the account. I gave the last hundred bucks to you.

I have an idea. How about I loan you a hundred bucks and you can pay me from that?

Yeah, that sounds like a good plan. I don't want to get in trouble from the Australian Agency for Fictional Characters.

I'll send some money through to you. I have your account details from when you sent me the money earlier.

Okay.

Did you get the money?

Yep.

EE NATIONAL BANK

NOTIFICATION OF TRANSFER

Amount: $100.00

Receipt Number: EENB 5142764894989

From: Tangentine P. Blockstock / 31599801

To: Tim Harris / 22816592

Date: 01 July 2020

Time: 6:42PM (AEST)

Okay, now send it back.

Okay.

Got it.

EE NATIONAL BANK

NOTIFICATION OF TRANSFER

Amount: $100.00

Receipt Number: EENB 5142764894990

From: Tim Harris / 22816592

To: Tangentine P. Blockstock / 31599801

Date: 01 July 2020

Time: 6:44PM (AEST)

Thanks for that. I owe you a hundred bucks.

No worries. Only happy to help out.

:)

I have an idea. Why don't you pay me back from one of your other bank accounts.

Of course! I should have thought of that before. I'll just open up the bank app again. I have another account linked to the first one and there is a hundred bucks in it!

Perfect! See, everything works out for a reason.

It sure does!

:)

Did you get it?

EE NATIONAL BANK

NOTIFICATION OF TRANSFER

Amount: $100.00

Receipt Number: EENB 514276489499l

From: Tim Harris / 29561822

To: Tangentine P. Blockstock / 31599801

Date: 01 July 2020

Time: 6:52PM (AEST)

•••

Great. That's a big weight off my mind.

Glad to hear it.

:)

Well, I had better get going, Tim.

Finally!

No need to be rude about it.

Sorry.

Thanks for helping me out. I'll text you later.

Bye!

●●●○○ EE4 7:02 PM 100%

E

EE National Bank

Message from CashBank:

You have reached the maximum daily transfer limit from your separate accounts. Your finances will be suspended until further notice.

SHORTCUT BURGERS

PREPARATION TIME: 60 minutes

COOKING TIME: 20 minutes

INGREDIENTS:

750g beef mince

1 cup of breadcrumbs

1 egg

1 onion

¼ cup of parsley, chopped

½ a lettuce, chopped

4 rashers of short cut bacon (That's not a bad idea, actually. Let's use some shortcuts.)

Don't worry about this ingredient.

You can get away without this one.

Not needed.

Also not needed.

Not worth the hassle.

Who needs a garnish?

METHOD:

1 Okay, let's be smart about this. Shortcuts are great. With that said, throw all the ingredients

into a bowl. But maybe leave the lettuce aside, as well as the short cut bacon.

2 The lettuce needs to be chopped. You could use a knife, but that would take too long. Dad's mowing the lawn outside. Idea! Shove the lettuce onto the end of a broom handle. Walk outside and hold the end of the broom under the lawnmower. Empty out the clippings catcher to collect the chopped lettuce. It doesn't really matter if any grass gets mixed up with the lettuce because it's green and tastes the same.

3 Use a blender to blend the ingredients in the bowl. Don't worry if the eggshell gets left in. Once it's blended, nobody will even know it's there.

4 To be honest, this is taking much longer than I had planned. Um… quickly make a few burger-sized bits of blah-blah-blah-blah! (Who has time for this? Life's too short!)

5 Speed up the cooking process by borrowing Dad's flamethrower. Hold it over each burger patty for a little while.

6 That'll do. (Blast! They're all burnt and on fire.)

7 Toss the burning patties into the pool. That'll put them out nice and fast.

8 Grab your skateboard and ride into town.

9 There's a shortcut through the alleyway that runs down behind the bowling club. Take it.

10 At the supermarket, run down to the freezer section and get one of those microwave hamburger thingies.

11 Pay at the express checkout.

12 Ride back home. Don't forget the shortcut.

13 Microwave the burger, but don't worry about taking it out of the packaging. (Okay, maybe that wasn't such a good idea. The plastic wrapping does tend to melt in the microwave.)

14 Hang on, let me think…

15 Got it! Ride back into town and head to the hamburger joint. They should have a drive-through.

16 Cut in on the car at the front of the line. I'm sure they won't mind.

17 Blast! I forgot to tell you to bring your wallet.

Start singing a song for the car next in the line. This is called busking, and you'll get money.

18 Maybe the car *will* mind that you pushed in. It's not likely they'll give you any money.

19 Ride home and look up home-delivery services on the internet. Find one that delivers burgers.

20 Order a burger.

21 Wait for the burger.

22 If it's taking too long, search for a packet of chips instead. You can get burger-flavoured chips. Hope for those.

23 That's it! Replace the burger with burger-flavoured chips. Genius.

24 The doorbell rings. It's the delivery guy with the burger. Tell him it would be more efficient if he ate the burger because you have a better plan.

25 Inform the delivery guy about the shortcut behind the bowling alley.

26 Send him on his way.

27 Search the pantry for burger-flavoured chips.

28 Search faster.

29 If you come up empty-handed, think about something quick and easy to make.

30 Burgers! Of course!

....

PREPARATION TIME: 60 minutes
COOKING TIME: 20 minutes
INGREDIENTS:

750g beef mince

1 cup of breadcrumbs

1 egg

1 onion

¼ cup of parsley, chopped

½ a lettuce, chopped

4 rashers of short cut bacon (That's not a bad idea, actually. Let's use some shortcuts.)

Don't worry about this ingredient.

You can get away without this one.

Not needed.

Also not needed.

Not worth the hassle.

Who needs a garnish?

You're probably feeling a strong sense of deja vu about all this…

PAGE WARS
2

IT IS A WELL-KNOWN FACT THAT THE LEFT PAGE IS FAR GREATER THAN THE RIGHT PAGE. THE LEFT PAGE IS, AND WILL ALWAYS BE, THE SUPERIOR SIDE OF A BOOK.

DON'T SAY THAT
I DIDN'T WARN YOU.

WARN ME ABOUT WHAT? WHAT ELSE COULD I POSSIBLY NEED TO KNOW ABOUT PARENTING? I AM THE MASTER OF ALL THINGS.

AAAARRRRGGGGHHHH!!!

NEWS

THE HORROR OF IT ALL!

NEWS

AH – THAT'S BETTER. NOTHING IS TOO HARD FOR ME. THE LEFT PAGE RULES AGAIN!

DON'T GET TOO FAR AHEAD OF YOURSELF. THERE IS SOMETHING YOU'VE OVERLOOKED.

MANY
YEARS
LATER

YOU NEVER DID TELL ME
THAT THING I OVERLOOKED.

YES, YES. THAT THING YOU OVERLOOKED. IT'S HAPPENING NOW. ENJOY, MY FRIEND.

WHAT ARE YOU DOING?
STOP IT AT ONCE!
I'M GOING THROUGH
A TEENAGE PHASE!

40
HE NEVER DOES LISTEN TO ME.
I KNEW THIS WOULD HAPPEN.

I WANT TO PLAY IN A HEAVY METAL BAND!
THE STRESS OF IT ALL! WHO WOULD HAVE THOUGHT TEENAGERS COULD BE SO MUCH TROUBLE?

HE-HE...

HA!

EEP
WHAT ARE YOU DOING?
STOP IT AT ONCE!

THAT'S MY BOY!

IT'S JUST A PHASE!

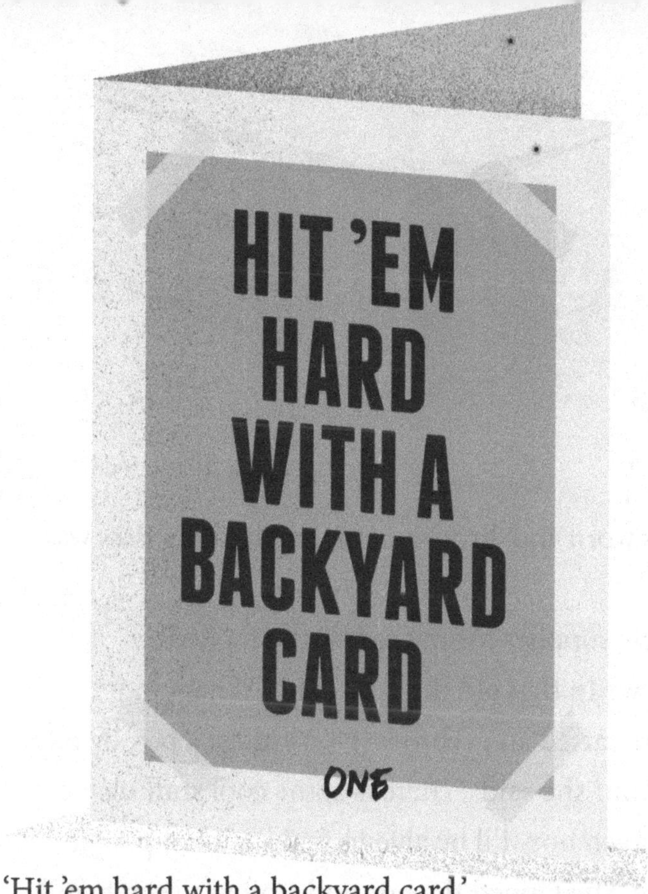

'Hit 'em hard with a backyard card.'

That's what Bess always says. Bess is my big sister, and she loves making cards. She makes them from scratch and hands them out all the time. Everybody says she is a kind soul. They say she has the special ability to cheer people up with her cards.

One day, Bess came home with a green box tucked under her arm. The box was tattered and torn, and the lid looked like it would fall off if a mouse sneezed.

'What's that?' I asked. I hadn't seen the box before.

It was worn and dirty – not the sort of thing Bess was into.

'New supplies for my cards,' she replied.

'New? In that old thing?' I said. 'What's in it?'

Bess raised an eyebrow. 'Don't judge a box by its lid, Tom,' she said. 'There is some cool stuff inside this green box. I'll be able to make a lot of people happy.' She tapped the box and smiled a secret smile.

Bess took the box straight out to the backyard and locked it in her work shed. Unfortunately for me, I wasn't allowed inside her work shed. It used to be Dad's old shed but, when he died, Mum let Bess have it for her card making.

That night at dinner, Bess told Mum about the box. I listened carefully because I wanted to find out more about it.

'I went to that funny craft store near the antique

shop today, Mum,' said Bess. 'The store is closing down, so everything was going cheap.'

Mum nodded to show she was listening.

'The lady who works there was very kind,' said Bess. 'She said she used to make cards and had just the things I needed to make my cards extra-special.'

'What's in that box?' I interrupted.

'You'll find out when I start making new cards.'

'I take it you bought some new supplies,' said Mum.

'The lady gave me the whole box for only ten dollars. She said my cards would really come to life.'

Bess didn't say much more about the lady or the store. She seemed to want to keep the whole thing quiet. I didn't bother asking any more questions. It was, after all, just an old green box.

TWO

Mum was hosting a special Sunday lunch. She was good like that. Ever since Dad died, she's made a big effort to reach out to any of her friends who might be feeling lonely, too. Her Sunday lunch was going to be a big event.

'Are you inviting Mrs Dredge?' I asked, hoping the answer would be no.

'Of course!' said Mum. 'She needs friends as much as anyone. She misses her husband.'

I frowned. 'Does that mean Danny is coming?'

'Yes.' She smiled. 'Perhaps you can sit next to him at lunch.'

Life had taken a bad turn. Danny Dredge was one of the nastiest kids in school. He was a known thief and bully. I was lucky I was in Year Four because he spent most of his time picking on the kids in his Year Six class. He had only been to our house once before, and had managed to steal my piggy bank, scribble his name on my bedroom wall in crayon, lose my pet frog and do something else I can't remember because it was so bad I blocked it from memory. I wasn't looking forward to the lunch. And I missed my frog.

'Don't worry,' said Bess. 'Show Mrs Dredge and Danny some kindness. Hit 'em hard with a backyard card!'

'I'm not into all that crafty stuff,' I sighed.

'Just leave it to me,' she said. 'This year, I have just the thing.' She smiled a secret smile and left the room. I remembered the green box.

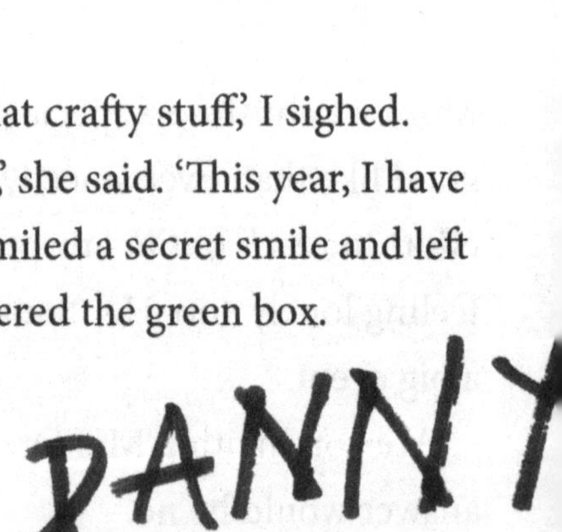

Sunday came around quickly, and I soon found myself standing at the front door waiting to greet the guests.

'Remember to be polite,' said Mum, brushing past me with a fruit tray.

'I will,' I said, though deep down I dreaded the thought of having lunch with Danny Dredge.

Danny and his mum were the first to arrive.

'Good afternoon, Tom,' said Mrs Dredge in a posh voice. She was wearing an expensive dress and she poked her nose in the air when she spoke. I had a good view of her nostrils and I could see that they were very clean.

'Good afternoon, Mrs Dredge,' I said politely. 'And good afternoon, Danny.'

Danny grunted something that sounded like 'not you again' and barged straight past me. He was much bigger than the last time he came over, and his voice sounded deeper. I was glad I didn't have any more pet frogs.

I showed Mrs Dredge to the living room, where Mum and Bess greeted her with a tray full of snacks. Danny was already munching on something that looked a lot like the cupcake I had been saving. How he found it so quickly, I'll never know. I mean,

who checks inside an old gumboot? To make things worse, Mum pointed down the hallway and told Danny to make himself at home in my bedroom.

Other guests started to arrive, and I had to go back to the front door. I could hear Danny clanging and banging about in my bedroom. Finally, after about fifteen minutes, I was free to rescue my stuff. I dashed down the hallway and into my room just in time to see Danny put my best racing car in his pocket.

'That's mine!' I cried. 'Give it back!'

'Make me,' said Danny, clenching his fists. His arms were huge. My toy car wasn't worth sacrificing my perfect chin for. I took a backwards step and told Danny that lunch was on.

Mum made the kids sit at their own table. Unfortunately for me, Danny and I were the only kids.

Danny didn't say much while we ate, but every now and then he kicked me in the shins to remind me he was there. Bess sat with the ladies at the main table and chatted to them. I kept looking at her for help, but every time she saw me, a secret smile would appear on her face. I wondered what she was up to.

After dessert, Mum told the guests that Bess had made something special for them. I wondered what Bess had made. I didn't notice Danny sneak away from the table and head back to my bedroom.

Bess stood up at one end of the table, holding a bunch of envelopes. 'I made you all a special card for today,' she said. 'Thank you for coming to our special Sunday lunch. We love having friends like you.'

'You are such a kind young lady,' said one of the guests. Another guest wiped a tear from her eye.

Mrs Dredge stared sternly at Bess, her nose in the air. She really did have clean nostrils.

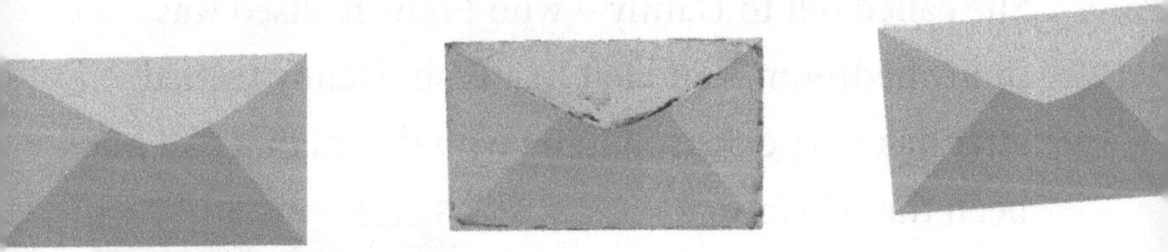

Bess put an envelope in front of each of the guests. I couldn't help but notice she put a tattered green envelope in front of Mrs Dredge. It reminded me of the old box. Mrs Dredge sniffed a posh sniff and picked up the envelope, tearing it open. All of the other guests smiled and opened theirs.

I was curious now. The envelope that Bess had given Mrs Dredge was the same colour as the green box. I craned my neck to see the card. I caught a quick glimpse of the front.

It was weird.

What was Bess thinking? On the front of Mrs Dredge's card, under a message that said 'YOU ARE SPECIAL', was a picture of a strange man. It wasn't even a picture of Mrs Dredge's dead husband. The man on the card was much taller and thinner. He was wearing a white shirt with red stripes. It was all a bit random.

That's all I had time to see because Mrs Dredge shoved the card into her purse and stood up to leave. She called out to Danny – who I now realised was in my bedroom – and left in a flash. Danny trotted after her, his pockets bulging with things that had not been there before.

Bess smiled a secret smile.

THREE

A few weeks later, something strange happened. I answered a knock at the front door to find

Mrs Dredge standing there. As usual, she was wearing an expensive dress, and I got another good view of her clean nostrils. But something was different this time. She was smiling. And there was a man with her. The man was tall and thin and he was wearing a white shirt with red stripes.

'Hello, young Tom,' said Mrs Dredge in the nicest voice I had ever heard her use.

'Hello.' I was surprised at her warmth.

'Is your lovely family home?'

'Um… yes,' I answered. 'Would you like to come inside?'

Mrs Dredge stepped inside. It was then I noticed she was holding hands with the man.

Mum and Bess appeared. Mum seemed surprised to see Mrs Dredge with the man. Bess didn't. She smiled secretly to herself.

Something strange was going on. Who was the man Mrs Dredge was with? There was something familiar about him, but I couldn't work out what it was.

We all sat down in the living room, and Mrs Dredge began to tell her story.

'It all started after that delightful Sunday lunch,' she said. 'Gorgeous Bess wrote in her exquisite card that I would find love again. I did not believe it at the time, and that's why I left so quickly.'

I saw a twinkle in Bess's eye.

Mrs Dredge continued. 'On the way home, I almost ran over an adorable puppy. I stopped the car and checked his dog tag.'

Bess beamed as Mrs Dredge told the story.

'The dog tag gave me an address, and I decided to return the puppy to his owner. I drove across town… And that's how I met Harry.'

She leaned over and kissed the man on the cheek.

'Gross,' I said.

'How lovely,' said Mum. 'We're very happy for you.'

'Thank you,' said Mrs Dredge. She grinned as she shared one more piece of information. 'Harry and I are getting married.'

'Congratulations!' cheered Mum and Bess at the same time.

I couldn't believe what I was hearing. Mrs Dredge, the rudest woman in town, was going to be married again. No wonder she was happy.

'Love knocked on my front door and I took it with both hands,' said the man. It was the first time he'd spoken, and I realised who he reminded me of – the man on the card.

'Hit 'em hard with a backyard card,' I whispered.

Bess heard me and smiled her secret smile.

'Where is Danny today?' asked Mum as we said goodbye to the guests.

'He's at home playing in his room,' she replied. 'I don't know where he gets his things from, but they sure make him happy!'

I frowned and remembered my missing things. Somehow, I had to get them back.

FOUR

Mum and Bess continued sharing kindness as though it was the most important thing in the world. It made me look bad in comparison. And I'm not that bad!

We arrived at church nice and early on the Sunday of the long weekend. Mum had made some chocolate cookies for the children, and she

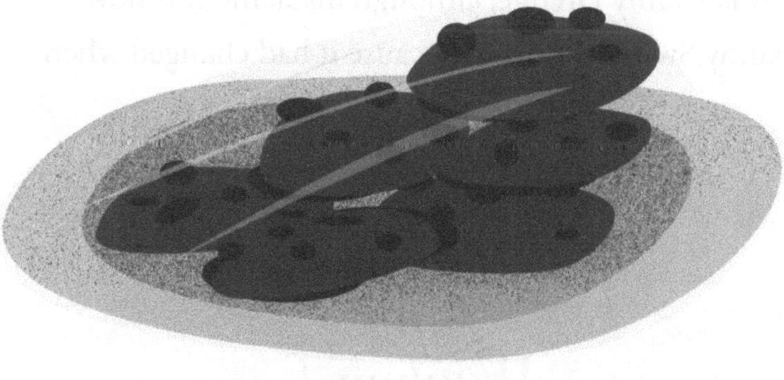

wanted to hand them out before the service.

'Those poor people,' said Mum, looking at a family sitting near the back. 'To think that Mr Bennett hasn't worked since last year. I don't know how they're surviving.'

Mum walked over to the Bennetts and gave the three kids a chocolate cookie each. They were very thankful. Bess followed Mum and gave one of her cards to the father. He smiled as he took the worn, green envelope. My curiosity was aroused as I remembered Bess's green box.

I watched as the man opened the card. I could just make out the front as he pulled it from the envelope. '*HAPPY LONG WEEKEND*' was written at the top, and there was a picture underneath of a man working on a car. I was just about to take a closer look when somebody stepped in front of me. It was Danny Dredge, although his name was now Danny Swindlebottom, because it had changed when

Mrs Dredge got married to Harry Swindlebottom.

'Got any more cookies?' he asked, towering over me. I'd heard about puberty, but this was ridiculous. Danny was even bigger than the last time I'd seen him. Plus, there was a pimple on his nose.

I shook my head, despite the fact I was holding a plate filled with cookies. I tried to ignore his pimple.

Danny snatched the plate from my hands. He demolished the contents in about twenty seconds and burped a loud burp. To make matters worse, he plonked himself next to me for the entire church service. Every now and then, he elbowed me in the ribs to remind me he was there.

At the end of the service, everyone went outside for morning tea. I tried to get away from Danny, but he followed me around.

'Got any more food?' he kept asking in a mean voice. 'Or should I say, "got any more toys"?' Then he'd chuckle.

Got any more pimples? I thought to myself. I was just about to work up the courage to ask if I could borrow some of my toys back, when a loud commotion erupted from the church car park. Everyone rushed outside to see what was going on. I managed to slip away from Danny and found myself at the front of the crowd.

Everyone was staring at the family who had been sitting at the back of church. The father was holding a piece of paper in his hands. There was a tear in his eye.

'I found this on my car seat,' he said, holding the paper for everyone to see. It was a job offer from the mechanic in town.

'I don't know how it got there,' said the man. 'But thank you to whoever put it there. Having a job will make a real difference to my family.'

I glanced at Bess. A tear ran down her cheek, too, and she smiled that same secret smile.

FIVE

A few weeks passed before I saw the next green envelope. It was for Mum's birthday. Mum had invited the Swindlebottoms over to celebrate, and I cooked a special birthday dinner – two-minute noodles.

'Hit 'em hard with a backyard card,' said Bess, handing Mum an old green envelope. My heart sped up as I recognised the type of card. It was a special one, and it must have come from the green box.

I had a good view of the card. It said '*HAPPY BIRTHDAY, MUM*' at the top. There was a beautiful

garden underneath, filled with colourful flowers. There were roses, tulips and daffodils. About a hundred violets made the shape of a smile. Mum read the message inside and thanked everyone for coming.

'What a delightful card,' said Mrs Swindlebottom who, since her wedding, had turned into the kindest lady in town.

'Got any more noodles?' grunted Danny who, since the wedding, was still the biggest idiot in town.

After dinner, Mum invited the adults to the living room for a cup of tea. Danny followed me back to my bedroom and started whacking me in the arm with one of my cricket stumps.

'I'm getting bored with your stuff,' he said. 'What else do you have?'

I gulped. His arms were twice as big as my neck, and I hated the idea of them meeting. I was powerless as he rummaged through my things, pocketing whatever he liked.

After he'd stuffed his pockets, he put his face close

to mine and sneered. 'Say one word to anybody and you're dead meat. These are *mine* now.'

I ignored his bad breath and nodded.

He pushed me in the chest and sent me crashing into my cupboard.

'I won't be so gentle next time.'

Something cheered me up the next morning. I woke to the sound of Mum and Bess talking excitedly.

'I've never seen such beautiful flowers,' said Mum. She was standing at the front door.

'Smell those lovely roses,' said Bess, who was smiling her secret smile. She winked at me.

'What happened?' I asked.

Bess pointed to the front garden.

What used to be just grass and weeds had turned into an amazing garden – overnight! The front yard was filled with colourful flowers. There were roses, tulips and daffodils, and about a hundred violets made the shape of a smile. It was exactly the same as the garden on Mum's card.

Mum didn't make the connection, but I did.

'Hit 'em hard with a backyard card,' I whispered.

Whatever was in that green box was doing something magical to the cards. First, Mrs Dredge's

Sunday-lunch card, then the job-offer card and now Mum's birthday card – they had all come true. The picture on the front had come to life.

'Do you have a card with a new phone on the front?' I joked. I had been asking Mum for one for weeks.

'Can you keep a secret?' said Bess. She sounded serious.

I was taken by surprise. 'Sure. You can trust me.'

Bess took me by the hand and led me straight to her work shed. I couldn't believe it. After all these years, I was about to see inside her shed.

'Promise you won't tell Mum,' she said.

'I promise.'

Bess unlocked the shed door, and I peered inside.

I was a bit disappointed by what I saw. I was expecting to see a giant cauldron or a wizard's hat or some crushed-up lizard guts. Her shed had none of

those. All it had was a small workbench, cluttered with card-making stuff.

'Is that all?'

Bess picked up an old green box at the edge of the bench.

'In here,' she said.

I opened the box. It was another disappointment.

'A blank card,' I said.

'Exactly,' said Bess. 'But it's a special blank card.'

'What do you mean?'

'The lady in the store said the cards come to life to cheer people up or give them help. I don't write anything in them or draw anything. The cards make themselves. All I have to do is choose who to give them to. When I give them to a person in need, they write and design themselves.'

'That's amazing,' I said. 'Just like Mum's birthday card.'

'Yep. I wasn't sure what Mum's card would do, but I'm glad it fixed the front garden. It's back to the way it used to be when Dad was still alive.'

I looked back inside the box, longing for there to be more than one card. Bess must have seen the disappointment on my face.

'It must go to someone who really needs it, Tom.'

'Can't you make more?' I asked. 'Can't you give it to me so I can get a new phone?'

'Sorry, Tom,' she said. 'The lady in the shop said that they can't be made again. This is the last one, and it has to go to someone in need.'

'So why are you telling me, then?'

'Because,' she grinned, 'I want you to tell me about Danny Swindlebottom.'

SIX

Christmas Day is a special occasion in our house. We always wake up early to give each other presents.

This year, I gave Bess some card-making stuff. She really liked it. I gave Mum a recipe book for two-minute noodle dishes. She said it was okay.

I couldn't believe my luck when Mum gave me

my gift. It was a phone! After months of pleading and asking, I finally got my wish. It was the best Christmas present ever.

'If you put it on to charge now, it should be ready to use this afternoon,' said Mum. 'Hurry, though, or we'll be late for church.'

I took my phone straight to my bedroom and plugged it in to the power point.

After church, the Swindlebottoms invited us around to their place for a special Christmas lunch. There was lots of yummy food, and Mum even sat between Danny and me. For once, he couldn't bash me to remind me he was there.

After lunch, Bess made an announcement.

'I have made special cards for everyone,' she said. 'Happy Christmas, and I hope you like them.'

Everyone got a red envelope and opened their cards at once. Everyone except for Danny, that is – his envelope was old and green. He shoved it into his pocket without even opening it.

I shot a glance at Bess. There was hope in her eyes. He had to open it sooner or later.

The adults started talking about boring stuff, and Danny invited me to his room.

To say there were a few of my toys in his room is

to say there were a few pimples on his face. His room was filled with my things. My remote-controlled car was on a shelf, my dinosaur puppet was under his bed, my collectable footy cards were scattered across the floor and my computer games were in his underwear drawer. Gross!

'This is all my stuff!' I protested.

'So what?' he chortled.

'It's stealing!'

'Wanna see what bashing is?'

I shook my head. It was no use. If I opened my mouth and told anyone, it would probably be the last time I would ever use my mouth at all.

I spent the rest of the afternoon dodging the tennis balls and shoes that Danny pelted at me. The only thing that kept me going was the thought of my brand-new phone.

After a few long hours, Mum finally took us home.

'How was your time with Danny?' she asked.

'I survived,' I said.

Bess gave me a secret look. 'Did he open…?'

'All he opened was a new can of tennis balls and some psychological scarring,' I said, shaking my head.

'Come on,' said Mum. 'He's not that bad, is he? Everyone needs a friend, Tom. I think it's wonderful that you spend time with Danny.'

'I guess so,' I said.

'Plus,' said Mum, 'tomorrow is a public holiday, and I've arranged for you to hang out with Danny again.'

SEVEN

We usually just sit around the day after Christmas, eating leftover food and watching the cricket on TV.

Not this time. As soon as I woke, I had to get ready to go back to the Swindlebottom's. Back to Danny's. Back to the bully.

At least I have my new phone, I thought. I put it in my pocket to remind me that things could be worse.

When we arrived at the Swindlebottom's, Mum did something unthinkable.

'Tom and Danny,' she said, 'Mr and Mrs Swindlebottom and Bess and I are going out for the day. We thought we would give you boys a special treat and let you stay here.'

'That's right,' said Mr Swindlebottom. 'We think you are grown-up enough to be trusted.'

My throat went dry and I couldn't think of anything to say. Could this really be happening?

Danny grunted. He trudged off to his bedroom and waved for me to follow.

'Go on,' said Mum. 'Have some fun!'

I looked to Bess for help, but she could only shrug. I was stuck. Stuck on my own with Danny Swindlebottom.

When we got to Danny's room, he slouched on his bed and gave me a menacing glare. I sat on the floor and tried not to listen to the car leave outside. I was stranded. There would be nobody to run to when

I started getting bashed and bruised. I gulped.

'Whadya get for Christmas?' asked Danny. 'Got any more toys?'

I shook my head. 'No.'

'Your mum said you got a new phone. Where is it?'

'Nowhere,' I said. 'I don't know what you're talking about.'

'Come on, Tommy boy,' he said. 'Give me your phone!'

'I don't have it!' I pleaded.

Danny held me by the throat. I coughed and spluttered and tried to break free. I kicked and struggled but he held on. He was too strong.

'Give me the phone!' he demanded.

'Let go,' I managed between gasps of air.

He let go for a moment, but only so he could grab my shirt, ripping it in the process. He shoved me against one of the shelves in his room.

'Fine then,' he snarled. 'You wanna play tough? I'll take it the *really* hard way.'

He thrust his hands into my pockets, kneeing me in the stomach as he did. I lost my breath and gave up the struggle. He took the phone and held it up triumphantly.

Then I did something foolish. I snatched the phone back.

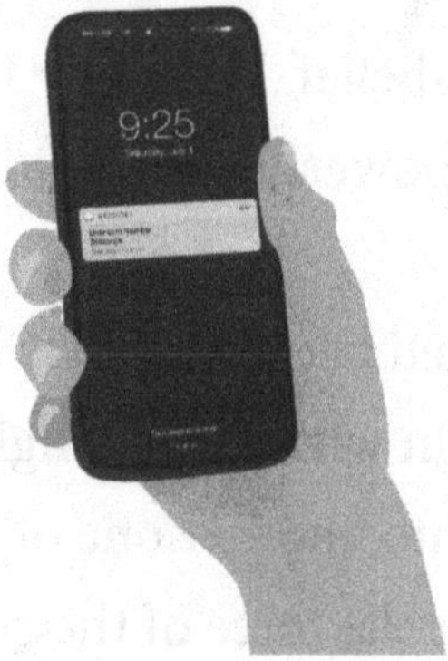

'It's mine!' I yelled. 'I got it for Christmas so leave it alone!'

Danny was angry. His whole face turned the colour of his pimples.

'You shouldn't have done that!'

He put his hands back around my neck and gripped tightly. This time, he was really choking me. I couldn't breathe at all. My arms thrashed about and knocked into the shelves behind me. I tried to feel for something to fight back with.

Danny laughed as he squeezed.

My hands fumbled over the toys.

Danny's grip got tighter, and I started seeing spots.

I clutched the first thing I could grip. It was flat and light, but it had to do.

I hit Danny over the head with it.

Danny screamed as he flew across the room, landing with a thud on the other side of his bed.

I stared in disbelief. Whatever I had in my hand was extremely powerful, but I didn't have time to see what it was.

Danny charged back at me. He looked ready to kill.

I hit him again with the flat, light thing and sent him crashing into another one of the shelves. They shattered under the force of the collision.

Danny lay there, panting and confused. Then his face filled with hate, and he charged back at me.

I defended myself yet again with the paper-like object, this time sending him flying through the bedroom door and smashing into the wall outside.

Danny groaned but, this time, he stayed down.

I looked down at the mystery object in my hand. It was an old, green envelope. It was the card from Bess, still unopened.

I opened the envelope and pulled out the card.

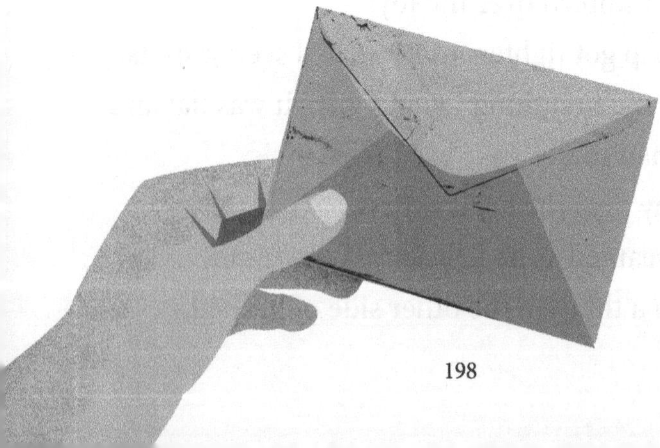

'*HAPPY BOXING DAY, TOM*!' was written at the top. Underneath was a picture of some boxing gloves.

I opened the card. It simply read:

Hit 'em hard with a backyard card. Love Bess.

PAGE WARS PART 3

IT IS A WELL-KNOWN FACT THAT THE LEFT PAGE IS FAR GREATER THAN THE RIGHT PAGE. THE LEFT PAGE IS, AND WILL ALWAYS BE, THE SUPERIOR SIDE OF A BOOK.

SIGH. HERE WE GO AGAIN.

FAREWELL, MY DEAR BOY.
BYE, DAD.

WHERE'S HE GOING?

HE'S ALWAYS WANTED
TO SEE THE WORLD.

OH.

IT'S JUST US, RIGHTY.

YEAH...

I'M THINKING ABOUT DOWNSIZING.

OH...

CAN I MOVE OVER TO YOUR PAGE? IT LOOKS LIKE A GOOD SIZE FOR ME.

BUT WHAT HAPPENED TO THE LEFT
PAGE BEING THE MOST SUPERIOR
SIDE OF A BOOK AND ALL THAT?

I WAS WRONG. YOU WERE RIGHT. YOU ARE RIGHT.

REALLY?

YEP.

COME ON OVER! YOU'LL LOVE IT HERE. THE RIGHT PAGE IS QUITE COMFORTABLE.

DEAR READER,
PLEASE TURN THE BOOK UPSIDE DOWN.
THANK YOU,
LEFTY
☺

IT IS A WELL-KNOWN FACT THAT
THE LEFT PAGE IS FAR GREATER
THAN THE RIGHT PAGE. THE LEFT
PAGE IS, AND WILL ALWAYS BE,
THE SUPERIOR SIDE OF A BOOK.

I. GIVE. UP.

●●○○ EE4 30%

7:40

Saturday 1 July

TANGENTINE TEXTS ONCE AGAIN

MESSAGES now

Unknown Number
iMessage
Turn page for more

Turn page to unlock

●●●○○ EE4
7:40 PM
30%
T
Tangentine
Today 7:40pm
SUP
Go away, Tangentine! I'm not going to reply to your texts.
Why?
Hello?
Today 7:55pm
SUP
SUP
SUP
SUP
SUP
Stop wasting your time.
SUP
SUP
SUP
SUP
SUP

I'm not going to write back.

You just did.

Ha!

I made you write back.

Sucker!

Hello?

Tim?

SUP

SUP

SUP

SUP

SUP

Today 9:05pm

SUP

SUP

SUP

SUP

yawn

Come on, Tim. Don't be like that.

Hello?

SUP

SUP

SUP

SUP

SUP

There's no point. I'm not going to engage in conversation with you.

The readers love it when you do.

I don't have any readers.

That's right.

I can't believe you forgot. You're always hounding me about not having any readers.

That's me.

Hello?

Are you still there?

SUP

SUP

SUP

SUP

SUP

SUP

SUP

WHAT DO YOU WANT?

Conversation.

Okay. I'll do it. I'll talk to you.

Yay!

So, what do you want to talk about?

Let me have a think...

Today 9:15pm

Think, Tim. What do you want to say?

Well, there is one thing I'd like to say.

What's that?

SUP

Delivered

READ ALL THE BOOKS IN THE EXPLODING ENDINGS SERIES

HAVE YOU READ THE MR BAMBUCKLE'S REMARKABLES SERIES?

... AND WHAT ABOUT THE TOFFLE TOWERS SERIES?

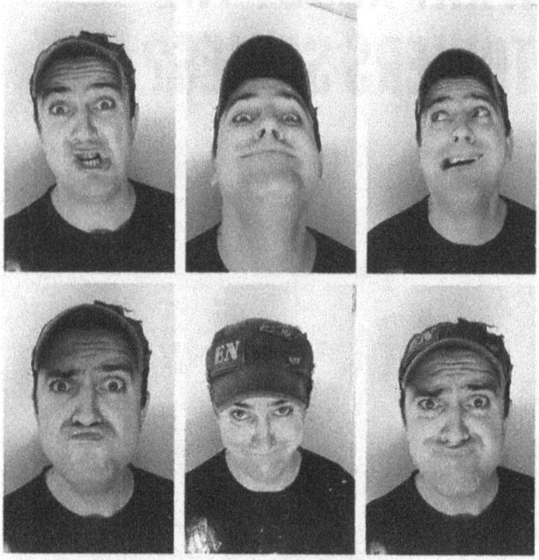

ABOUT TIM HARRIS

Tim Harris is the bestselling author of several laugh-out-loud series for kids, including Toffle Towers, Mr Bambuckle's Remarkables and Exploding Endings.

A former primary school teacher of fifteen years, his stories are filled with quirky scenarios, loveable characters and plenty of imagination. Tim's 'humour with heart' writing style has seen his books receive multiple awards, including two KOALA Honour Books (2017 and 2019) and a Children's Book